RYLAN JOHN CAVELL

VIOLENCE

and

LAVENDER

Locations, characters and situations depicted within the snug pages of this novel are all fictitious, though inspired by the real world as it was experienced by its Queer population during the 1920's.

Consider the Manchester in this book to be 'reality-adjacent'.

Dedicated to my darling husband-to-be Johnny

With special thanks to the marvellous chaps of *Fambles*

Love and hugs x

Chapter One.   *It Starts With A Ghost In A Window.*

Chapter Two.   *Messages.*

Chapter Three.   *Justice.*

Chapter Four.   *New Evidence.*

Chapter Five.   *What The Whisperers Heard.*

Chapter Six.   *Madame Miasma.*

Chapter Seven.   *Merry Belles and Prison Cells.*

Chapter Eight.   *His Beloved Mother.*

Chapter Nine.   *Mirrors.*

Chapter Ten.   *Mr Nettle.*

Chapter Eleven.   *A Sitting Ducky.*

Chapter Twelve.   *A New Room Mate.*

Chapter One

It Starts With A Ghost In A Window

The boy who snored loudly in the bed across from mine will snore no more. Losing a friend so suddenly, and so viciously leaves a void in the heart. I have felt muggy-headed and untethered since I heard the news. The world has been turning without me, and at any moment I could be caught by a breeze and scattered into pieces. As usual a chain of Whisperers allowed us to know the grisly story before it became public knowledge, when it was published in prudishly scant detail in the final edition of the Evening News paper. I had read the article askance, shocked to my core that the person those lines of rigid little letters spoke of was my dear friend.

It is the morning of his funeral. My bijou abode is bare and cold. I brush down my best suit, slip into it and hurry from the room, pulling on my thick woollen overcoat and jamming my second-hand Homburg hat over my hair. I lock the door and descend the staircase lightly, not trusting the wooden steps to last the winter. Something has come loose on the roof again, and a thin column of rain cascades down the centre of the stairwell. Mrs Taffeta the Landlady attempts to engage me in gossip as I leave. I swerve her, simply saying, "It's raining inside again."

I do not own an umbrella, and so I must tolerate the many forms of rain unique to Manchester. I pause before moving away from the front door of the communal building, and cast my eyes up, "Did I lock the door?

Of course I did. My gaze rises to the window of my little room high above; a dirty squinting eye in the face of the building. The curtain moves. I scowl, and take a step back, the better to see into the room. I bump into a passing lady and apologise. She tuts at me and hurries on her way. My attention is on the window above, there is movement there. Then a light. Someone has turned on the light in my room! While I stand looking up, rain hitting my face, I examine how brave I am feeling. I should return to the room and discover the identity of this invader into my private sanctum.

I *should*. But my feet are rooted to the spot, and my mouth hangs open, as the curtain high above me is tweaked to one side. Standing in the window is my former roommate. The recently deceased Lawrence Clifford DeVeire. He looks sad. He catches sight of me and he grins one of his charming, lopsided smiles. He waves enthusiastically, and I wave back dumbfounded.

This is impossible. He is dead. Very dead indeed. I run back into the building past Mrs Taffeta and up the stairs, taking them two and three at a time, bounding as fast as I can to see my friend! I pant heavily as I fumble with the key, unlocking the door. I knock it open and stumble into darkness beyond. The electric wall light is off, the curtain is closed, and my friend is of course absent. I sag onto my thin bed.

"Stop being silly, Rowan." I chide myself for such a flight of fancy, "Wishful thinking. That's all it is."My friend is dead. He is very dead indeed, and no silly delusion will bring him back. I am not sure what I have seen, and I do not believe in ghosts, but the moment of joy it gave me; the possibility of seeing my friend once more, leaves a deeper hollow in my heart as it fades.

Before I leave again, I pull the curtain to one side, and pinch the cigarette-stained netting up to the frame. The glass is wet with condensation. I sigh, running a finger across the smooth pane, drawing a happy face. My own features are hung, reflected unhappily back at me. The void within is deepening, making me feel as cold inside as the weather is without. I have a funeral to attend, and so I depart, locking the door securely behind me.

The family to which my dear friend belonged is one of the country's more well-to-do dynasties. They come complete with flared nostrils, pallid cheeks, unsettling paunch, and wet eyes. They display all the traits of creatures more at home with skulking under rocks, flicking forked tongues, than entertaining in polite society. We watch from a safe distance.

The rain finally abates as the coffin is lowered into the recently dug hole in the midst of the family huddle of umbrellas and repressed emotion. I can smell the freshly overturned layers of history, the heavy aroma of ancient burials and recent decorative landscaping.

Lady Nell stands to my left, wearing large dark glasses despite the dim light of this overcast day. She may call herself a Lady, but the title is purely for effect. She styles herself in a thoroughly modern way, even today while she wears her more somber attire. Her pencil dress is entirely hidden by her fur-trimmed coat, which starts at her chin and finishes just below the knee. Her hair is cut into a wavy bob, and she clutches a small bag, from which she pulls a compact, and examines her reflection for a moment. How she can see herself through the dark glasses I do not know. She adjusts the angle of the felt cap on her head, and closes the compact with a dramatic flourish.

Edgar, suited smartly as ever, has his arm looped through the crook of hers, holding a large umbrella to shelter them both by. He is a good deal shorter than Lady Nell, and so his arm is stretched up high to ensure they both remain covered by the canvas canopy.

My hat and overcoat are dripping, beneath which I remain mostly, but not entirely dry. I consider telling them about the vision in the window, but decide against it. It was clearly a product of my grief-stricken imagination.

We look an odd trio, Lady Nell stands particularly tall for a typical woman and is thin as a rake, everything about her appears dainty. Edgar is pale and as wide as he is tall, with dark locks slicked back on his head. From the corner of his crooked mouth hangs a thick and pungent cigar. His face is deeply lined, and highly animated. One eyebrow is permanently arched from years of training above a monocle.

Then there is myself, with my own peculiarities. We are related not by blood, but by our shared differences, and a camaraderie that we find lacking elsewhere.

The graveyard is vast, and undulates gently over a

series of small man-made hills. Trees grow here and there amid the lines of graves. We stand beside the leafless body of an old Oak. Winter has robbed it of its summer gown, scattering it in brown tatters across the grass underfoot. In summer this is a favoured picnic destination for the well-to-do of the city. I have always found such a past time rather peculiar.

I feel a tear prick at the corner of my eye. Edgar hands me one of his monogrammed handkerchiefs, and I dry my eyes. We three knew the Dear Departed better than his family ever did, and yet we are the ones forced to grieve from a distance. It is the way of things, I suppose. We are considered unsavoury. To be seen weeping alongside such a family as the DeVeires would likely cause some form of social scandal.

That would suit Lady Nell very well, scandal is her byword for having a lovely time. That would not suit the De-Veires however, and one of the party seems intent on making that plain. I notice this broad-shouldered gentleman repeatedly glaring at us.

"We're in for trouble." I say softly.

Lady Nell tuts, "Sure as eggs."

Removing a hip flask from her clutch bag, she takes a long swig. Without offering it to either of us, she tucks it away. The smell of the neat gin is enough for me. I have never been a big drinker.

"it's all a bit much, isn't it? All this melodrama, it's all a show." Edgar remarks at the funeral party, taking a puff on his cigar.

A little distance away stands the horse-drawn hearse, resplendent in black ostrich plumes. Forming a semi-circle outside of the family are the professional mourners. These men and women wear finely tailored black clothing, and some men hold tall staffs wrapped in black fabric. These mourners put their all into weeping and sobbing, so that the family can maintain their stoney-faced emotional disconnection, and stiff upper lips.

The vicar finishes his duties, shakes the correct hands, pats ladies with veiled faces on the shoulder, and departs. The family and mourners break into small clusters, beginning to drift away, following the Man Of God.

The broad-shouldered gentleman remains. After staring at us for a good long while, he makes his way up the incline toward us. As he draws closer, I can see that his cheeks are rouged with blood and fury. His right hand is a fist around his decorative walking cane, and his jaw is set firm.

Beside me, I detect Nell imperceptibly tense. She does not move, or alter her position, yet something in her demeanour shifts and becomes more solid.

The approaching man stops striding only when he finds himself within arms reach of us. A moment more and I would have had to choose between fighting him off or running from him.

"Can we help you?" Lady Nell asks calmly.

The man is balding, and has a hard countenance. His

is a face made for arguments, forged in a boxing ring. One ear is mildly cauliflowered, and he holds his arms bent a fraction at the elbows. The better to strike a blow with, I suspect.

Despite his looks he is still a Gentleman, and as such, breeding and society will not allow him to bellow and rage against a lady in such a public place, nor in front of family members who may be lingering nearby. It would be uncouth.

"You can explain why you are here." His voice is flushed with emotion, and cracks as he speaks. Whether it is due to the anger I see in his eyes, or sorrow for the deceased I can not tell.

"We have as much right to mourn the boy as you."

Edgar gesticulates towards the grave, the cigar in his hand leaving grey smoke trails wafting back and forth.

The four men whose job it was to lower the coffin into the grave are now putting their backs into the job of filling in the hole. I wipe a tear from my eye once more. The poor boy, laid to rest due to such horrible events.

The angry man in front of us huffs noisily, shaking his head, "You have no right to be here, you hear me? None whatsoever. I don't believe your sort have the emotional range to understand the loss we are feeling as a family."

Lady Nell smiles tartly, her lips pouting as she replies, "Our *sort*? Whatever might you mean?"

"Disgusting. Soulless. Hedonistic vermin."

Lady Nell laughs loudly in the man's face, throwing

13

her head back. He seems genuinely taken aback by her reaction. The surprise is fleeting.

He takes one more step forward, jabbing a finger under Edgar's nose, "You listen here, if I weren't a Gentleman I'd lay you out right here for simply showing your face."

The brash intrusion into his personal space causes Edgar to drop his cigar, and for the umbrella to wobble dangerously around. Lady Nell, quick as a flash moves forward, knocking the man back by three paces. She advances on him, tense and sharp as a knife.

"You are no Gentleman, *sir*." She hisses, "If you wish to strike someone, do so! But strike me." She removes her dark glasses, revealing tear-stained makeup and one enormous purple bruise around her left eye, "You won't be the first, you won't be the last. This one thing I can guarantee you; Each time, I come out on top."

Lady Nell may well be thin as a bean pole, but she is hard as steel. I feel quite useless. My reactions are not as fast as Nell's, and my resolve not as strong as Edgar's. I am scared of this man.

He ignores me, and glares at the woman who has dared to talk back to him. She stands a good head taller, and as she stares her icy blue eyes into his, it seems as if she is looking into his very soul. Whatever she sees there does not please her.

There is an electric tension between them, as neither want to be the first to look away, or to show a sign of weakness.

"Go to your family, Mr DeVeire." I manage to say, "I am sure they will be in need of comfort."

Removing his attention from Nell breaks the stalemate.

"What queer company my brother kept. A faggot, a slut and a bastard." He looks us up and down, sneering.

"Which of us is which, do you think?" Lady Nell asks Edgar and me. She pushes the dark glasses back into place on her face, and plumps up the fur collar of her coat, "I hope I'm the slut." She smirks.

Outraged, and with his face reddening rapidly, the man confronting us huffs and puffs. An elderly lady calls in our direction, summoning the angry man away.

He barks a warning at us to stay clear of his family, then turns to go. Once he has departed, Lady Nell sighs a deep, relieved sigh.

"He never mentioned having a brother." I say of the Dear Departed.

"He kept his cards close to his chest, that boy" Edgar replies, closing the umbrella, then stooping to retrieve his cigar from the damp grass, "Ruined." he grumbles, discarding it.

I stare across the graveyard to the freshly turned oblong of soil being laid upon our friend's coffin. Two weeks ago I spoke with the Dear Departed last. Now I have seen him buried. How a young life could be snuffed out so suddenly wrecked me to the core. I could not understand how anyone could have done to him the vile things that had ended his life.

"Shall we?" I ask, looking to my two friends.

Edgar nods, and we three move forward as one. The grass and leaves squelch underfoot. A mist of drizzle hangs in the air, and the gentle wind bites at my nose and exposed fingers. I forgot to wear my gloves.

The gravestone is not yet in place, and no doubt it will be as gaudy as the other monuments placed upon graves by moneyed families.

"We miss you, Lawrence." I say.

Lady Nell allows herself a gentle sob, holding her gloved hands to her mouth. Edgar, usually so stoic, has the hint of a quivering lip, clutching the curved handle of his umbrella so tight his fingers are white.

We did not come here empty handed. We each of us wear a sprig of meaningful flowers, these we intend to lay at the grave, and we do so, one by one. Three stems of bright lavender lay on the freshly turned soil.

We hug each other in a tight huddle. Lady Nell's long arms wrapping around Edgar and myself, pulling us tightly to her bosom.

"Enough of this." Edgar says after a few moments, "Sobbing will do us no good."

"A release for the soul." Nell breathes, "And it is doing *me* a power of good." She smiles awkwardly at us, before taking another long sip from her hip flask.

Edgar points at the small silver vessel, "Now that, my good woman, is a very fine idea."

16

Without a word, we agree to retire to our favoured watering hole, for the drinking of a toast to the Dear Departed, and to drown our woes.

CHAPTER TWO

MESSAGES

The watering hole in question is owned and loosely run by Lady Nell. The entrance to this well-known-to-only-those-who-need-to-know grotto can be found at the end of a narrow alley behind a butchers and a locksmiths. The canal is not far away, and the shouts of workmen in the surrounding warehouses drift on the chill air to our ears.

Down the narrow alley, an even narrower wooden staircase leads up to the spine-like rooftops of the fourth floor, where the highest rooms of several buildings have been knocked through, creating a large, vaulted space.

Beams and rafters criss-cross here and there, and between them are arranged tables and chairs. Everywhere there hangs red fabric and golden tassels. Thin cushions lay on the seats and piled in corners on the floor. Cracked portraits of a younger Nell hang on the wall behind the small bar, and the solitary window looks out from above the rickety stage to a cloudy grey sky.

This early in the day we expect to find the barman serving a smattering of regulars who have not found their way home from the night before. Today however it seems that many people came upon the same idea as ourselves.

"To the Dear Departed!" The rooftops ring, as the occupants of the crowded room sink a short glass of Lady Nell's bathtub-brewed gin in unison. There follow the usual hisses and gasps that accompany the consumption of said gin.

"It'll put hairs on your chest," She chuckles, nudging me in the ribs, "Trust me, I should know!"

I rest my empty glass on the nearest tabletop and try to breath slowly. I feel queasy, and fear the spirit may well come back to haunt me, and the floor, and anyone within spitting distance.

I smile at Lady Nell, pretending to be in less discomfort than I am. She pats me on the back, before moving off into the crowd.

Having shed her coat, Nell's drop-waist frock is a marked contrast to the grey feeling of the day. It is a pale spearmint, with a beading of faux pearls and decorative fringing at the hem in the style of a Flapper. She shimmers amongst the throng, relishing the distraction from the unhappy event that morning.

Body heat from the clustered people makes me feel stifled. I begin to sweat, and I pull at my collar to loosen it. I am uncomfortable in this jovial melee, and in these clothes which are still a little moist.

Stumbling over a woman lay sleeping on the floor, I leave Nell's Place and close the door behind me. The chill of November is refreshing, but equally is unpleasant. The damp smell from the canal and dingy back alleys overpower the bunches of posies scattered about the place. These are Nell's attempt to introduce a more pleasing fragrance to her small rooftop fiefdom. She has been wholly unsuccessful.

I hear the door open and close behind me as Edgar

joins me on the stairs. Standing at my side, he swings his umbrella up to rest on his left shoulder. He has acquired a bowler hat from somewhere, and it sits at an angle on his square skull.

"Suit me?" He asks.

"It's a little small."

"I like it."

"What will happen now?"

Edgar turns to face me.

"We continue. We carry on doing what we have always done, but without him."

I tut, as he has not fully understood my meaning.

"About his murder." I say.

"Ahh." Edgar frowns with one eyebrow, "I couldn't possibly say, ducky."

"The police-"

He cuts me off with a wave of his free hand, "We can't get ourselves involved with any investigation. Hilda Handcuffs asks too many questions, the answers to which will lead to you, me, and Nell. Not to mention a great many others who could do without the Constabulary nosing about their business."

I'm at a loose end. He can see it in my face.

"I'm sorry." He says, "It's just how it is."

"I don't want to go home." I say after a long pause. I do not admit that this is due to the apparition at my window. No doubt Edgar makes his own mind up as to why this might be.

"I understand. Look..." he rests a hand on my upper arm, "It is terrible. But it is not the first time something like this has occurred to one of us. I doubt very much it will be the last either." His hand drops, and his eyes cast their gaze across the rooftops and smoking chimney stacks, "We continue. What else can we do?"

Nothing.

We all know how the world works; against us.

"I must away. Keep your pecker up." He smiles at me, a kindly wrinkle at the side of his eye.

I watch as he trots down the wooden staircase and saunters away down the alley. I bubble angrily at him for a moment. It's all well and good for Edgar; he is rich, has a grand house and wants for nothing. Not like the rest of us who scrape through life on meagre wages and handouts, or the kindness of friends and strangers, ever wary that the next body fished from the canal might be ours, or that the police might decide that we look better in shades of black and blue.

But Edgar too lives on a knife's edge, I remind myself, albeit a different blade than mine or Nell's, and my anger goes off the boil.

I dally there, at the top of that flight of stairs. The idea of returning home is too distressing; that empty unmade bed across the room from mine.

The Dear Departed and myself lived in each other's pockets for much of the preceding eleven months. I find myself gazing with unfocused eyes into the middle distance. I look at nothing in particular, allowing the scene before me to

21

be a blotchy watercolour of slowly swirling grey and brown.

I contemplate returning to the wake and drinking another short glass of Nell's bathtub gin. I can still feel the volatile bitter liquid on the rear of my tongue and lining my throat, which tells me that what I drank was more than enough. I return briefly to retrieve my hat and overcoat, before slipping away.

I make my way through the city streets, crookedly lined with little shops, bakeries, cafes, butchers and green-grocers. At this time of day, the latter are in good voice, filling the streets with cries declaring the price of potatoes, leeks and other sundry items. This old area of town, squashed between the Rochdale Canal and tall imposing warehouses, has a personality split in two by the rise and fall of the sun. During the day it is hard working, respectable, full of polite nods and gracious behaviour.

It is not a well-to-do area, the middle class visit for a taste of the earthy life of the working man, rubbing shoulders with the household staff of the upper class, visiting to purchase the food, linen and services needed to maintain the large townhouses in which they are employed.

Errand boys dash here and there, and if it wasn't for the distant coughing of an occasional motorcar and the rattling of the trams, you could very well believe that we still live in some simpler bygone era.

I pause to watch a young man pasting a poster for a new Motion Picture over the boarded-up window of a long-dead apothecary shop. Human Desires, it proclaims, will thrill the audience. I have no doubt it will.

I contemplate how it is perhaps the desires of humans that change as the sun sets, rather than the city itself.

The everyday, run-of-the-mill businesses lock their doors. The proprietors retire for their evening meals, to warm their feet by open fires.

One door closes, and another opens.

Where you may not have noticed a door, or a little window during the day, now there is one. Now there is a light behind the glass. Now there is a sign up above the door. Now the other side of the personality is shown. Now a selection of more basic human desires awaken, and are catered to.

But it is barely past midday, and those more at home under the care of the moon are hidden. Yet I can see the doors and windows and alleys and places that come alive under Luna's silvery light hidden in plain sight. They are shrouded; obscured by stalls and the toing and froing of people.

I recall the various escapades the Dear Departed and myself engaged in, giggling and full of mischief. One memorable evening we stole the hat of a careless sleeping Policeman. Using a discarded broom, we hooked it onto a disused gas street lamp. We then hid, and flicked stones at the man until he awoke. Watching him jump and struggle, failing to reclaim his pilfered hat caused us to guffaw loudly from our hiding place. This gave us away, and were chased by the furious Officer for some twenty minutes until we lost him in the twisting streets.

23

I smile to myself. Thinking of the happy times we shared, the frolics we engaged in, and the warmth of our affection help me shift a little of my lingering gloom. It is time to brave returning to the room we called ours, which is now mine alone.

I amble through the familiar streets, in no great hurry, but not dawdling either. I turn a corner, stepping quickly aside to avoid the stream of piss being let forth by a stray dog. I trip slightly on a loose cobble, and stumble into someone. I apologise profusely and immediately.

The individual to which I find myself in extremely close proximity smiles at me warmly, and hugs me. The embrace takes me by surprise, and I stiffen.

To be seen in the embrace of another man could land me under the penetrating gaze of the rozzers. I pull away quickly, thanking him for catching me and saving me from the fall. I say this a little louder than expected, and hope that anyone who was witness to the embrace would be mollified by this, and move on.

Before me is a friend of the Dear Departed. A disreputable omi-palone by the name of Oddly Brown. Upon being described as such by a regular John, he took the comment as his name in jest. It stuck. Now no one can remember what his name truly is.

I know that he hails from the Americas, but his family is not of European origin. He is one of those indigenous to the New World. His hair is long and black, his skin maintains a beautiful sun-kissed glow, and his eyes are as bright as his smile.

"It is good to see you." He beams at me.

I respond in kind, and we engage in some idle chatter. I do not know him overly well, yet we talk without pause, and he makes me laugh. He falters for a moment.

"Yes?" I ask, wary of the approaching sentence.

"How was the funeral?"

I perform some mental gymnastics as I attempt to find a way to describe the events of the morning without becoming too morose. I vault, balance, and finally I fall on my face, "I cried." I say.

Oddly nods and moves to pull me into a tight bear hug. I react quickly enough to stop it before it occurs.

He may not be wary of curious glances from passers by, but I am. I appreciate the gesture, but the time and place are all wrong. Besides which, I do not particularly like the overpowering cologne he has apparently bathed in. It is likely a gift from a regular client. I pull away but he hangs onto my wrists, clutching me tightly, and affectionately.

"I'm heading home now. I need to tidy away his belongings and similar such things." I say.

A curious look crosses Oddly's face, and he lets go of me slowly.

"What is it?" I ask.

"When last you spoke with Lawrie, how did he seem?" He bites his lip.

I think back to my final encounter with the Dear Departed. It had been unremarkable. He had seemed himself;

affable, charming and busy, "No change from the usual. Why?"

Oddly speaks now in lower tones, almost whispering, "Last I spoke with him, he didn't say much. He was so scared."

Scared?

I had never seen him scared. He always appeared unflappable. In all the scrapes we had found ourselves in, a jovial comment and cheeky wink always enabled us to avoid severe repercussions.

Clearly Oddly wants to say more, and I attempt to push on with this conversation. It is cut short however by a shout from amongst the nearby crowd.

"Bugger." Oddly says, then melts away into the bustle of the day.

As well as being a boy for hire, he is also a pickpocket, trickster, and all-round scamp. No doubt the shout emanated from the throat of someone discovering their pocket watch or change purse missing. Oddly is a master of sleight-of-hand and misdirection.

Perturbed by his comment of the fear he saw in the Dear Departed before his demise, I meander homeward, my mind turning over the horrible possibilities again and again.

Shaking away such dreadful thoughts, I come to the realisation that I have walked well past my own abode. Turning around and walking back to the small door, I fish in my pocket for the key.

I let myself in the outer door, and begin to climb the

stairs beyond, narrowly avoiding yet another banal conversation with Mrs Taffeta. The stairway is narrow, rickety, and my feet tread lightly.

Each room of the building is currently let, and though there are many people cohabiting in this rather narrow slice of Manchester, I have never seen a single one of them. Though I have frequently found it necessary to wait for a young woman known as Tiffin to vacate the shared bathroom. I do not know what it is she does that takes so long, but she does it very noisily.

As I climb higher, step by slow step approaching my door a knot pulls itself around my stomach. I pause for a moment, as I breathe deeply to calm my nerves. I am alarmed when I notice the door to our... my room is ajar. I did not leave it that way. I made sure I locked it. Yes, I definitely locked it.

Immobile on the final step, I feel myself swaying on the spot. My hand on the bannister grips tighter. I dare not close my eyes, I dare not breathe. Is there someone in there? An intruder determined to steal whatever items of minuscule value lay within, perhaps? For a moment I imagine the Dear Departed laid back on his bed, that lopsided smirk on his angular face, laughing at me for falling for such an obvious jape. The whole thing was an elaborate ruse!

This is a whimsy, and impossible.

He is quite quite dead.

Yet the vision in the window returns to my thoughts. Having been absent from the room for most of the morning,

I hope that whoever broke in must be long gone by now. I find this to be true.

I push the door open and it creaks; the pitch and tone identical to when last I had heard it. The room is in darkness as I reach for the light switch. The single electric wall-mounted light clicks into life, shining dimly through a frosted glass shade decorated with etched flowers. The blooms are cast as indistinct bright patches onto the walls which still hold their aged wallpaper.

The red armchair remains covered with a crocheted blanket of black and blue wool. The beds are still matchstick thin and heaped with old bedclothes. The writing desk and doorless wardrobe still stand either side of the small window, rectangular gargoyles guarding the rooftop view.

As with Lady Nell's bar, this room sits at eye level with the pointed roofs and solid brick chimneys of the city.

I pull aside the heavy green curtain to see the cigarette-smoke stained netting is pinched to one side as I had left it, and the window is shut and locked. There is still a faint smudge of the smiling face I drew on the pane a few hours before.

Everything seems in order. There is no sign of any intrusion into this corner of the world I call my home. Confused, I reexamine the room.

Why would someone break in and not move or steal anything? I step out onto the landing and call down the stairs to Mrs Taffeta, "Has anyone been up into my room today?"

I wait for her shuffling feet to bring her into view,

looking up at me with her small dark eyes, "Not as far as I know." She calls up, "Will you be wanting any tea doing? I know it'll have been a *very* trying day."

I find myself stunned into silence. Mrs Taffeta has never before offered to make me any food. She guards her small kitchen as a dragon guards its gold.

"No. Thank you, though."

I return to my room before she can continue the conversation. I double and triple check. It is as untidy as I left it, with nothing noticeably altered or absent.

"Perhaps I didn't lock the door after all."

My head is a muddle. I try to focus, and to shake off a creeping cold fear, whose fingers are lightly brushing the nape of my neck. I must gather together the belongings of the Dear Departed.

Many questions as to what to do with the belongings dance merrily around my head while I tidy. I operate automatically and with blank eyes.

Being the very slightly clumsy person I am, while carrying a small pile of dogeared novellas, I trip over an ashtray left carelessly on the floor, and fall into the armchair while facing the wrong way. Fag ends and ash cascade across the room, and I curse loudly.

It is painful and uncomfortable to be bent the wrong way in this chair, and I let the books go to push myself upright. As I do so, my hand eases into the space between the seat and back of the chair. Through the wool of the crocheted blanket my fingers close on something that I do not expect to be there.

Once I put myself into a stable upright position, and place the novellas to one side, I pull away the blanket and slowly push my fingers into the space once again. My fingertips close on sheaves of paper. Lots of folded paper. I pull them out, and discover handwritten letters.

Amongst these letters I identify the handwriting of at least two people. I sit in the chair, no longer caring for the cigarette mess littering the floor. The envelopes are all opened, with the letters snugly nestled within.

"Why did you hide these?" I ask the Dear Departed.

"I was scared." He replies.

"Scared of what?" I cannot help but ask.

It is at this precise moment the hand of creeping cold fear grabs me around the throat. A dread terror that makes me choke for breath, and makes my hands and knees quiver. I dare not look up from the paper in my hand. It looks expensive stationary and my eyes bore into the centre of the D in his surname upon the top-most envelope. I cannot blink. I cannot breathe. In front of me the Dear Departed rests on his haunches, placing a hand on each of the armchairs wide arms.

"Look at me." he says softly.

I shake my head. His voice is warm and friendly yet I did not dare look up, "You are not really here. This is my imagination."

He laughs at me, and slaps my left knee playfully. "Did that feel like your imagination?"

"No." I say, my voice small, "But you died."

"Yes."

In my peripheral vision I can see him smiling at me, that one sided smile I thought so endearing. He wears his dark blue corduroy suit, and his shirt is open at the neck.

"You were buried." I say.

"Yes."

"In a coffin."

"As is the usual way."

I stammer, my jaw flapping, unsure what I should say to him next. I am still staring at the D in DeVeire, building the courage to look up.

"You're not safe." He says, a concerned tone to his voice.

Now I look up. I move my eyes swiftly to look into his, but they are not there.

He is not there.

I am alone in the room, and it is cold, and ever so empty. As I sit here, my eyes filling with thick tears, I begin to shiver. It is not the cold that forces this reaction, it is something inside me; some deep emotional reaction.

"I think I'm going mad." I rub my eyes, breathing deeply, feeling silly.

Ghosts are not real' I think to myself, repeating this again and again for several minutes. My shaking fingers are playing about the edges of the letters as I shuffle them absentmindedly like a large deck of cards. I select one at random. I lay the others on my lap, and gently tug the letter from its envelope.

It is a single piece of paper folded in three. The handwriting is neat and curved. The *t* are tall, and the *s* are fat. It is signed 'Beloved Mother'.

The details of the letter are inconsequential; distant family feuds, unsuitable marriages, the health of several pets in fine detail, with helpful disgusting doodle. Not wanting to read any more than I already have about the dirty end of a poorly Spaniel, I return the letter to its envelope.

Only now do I detect a slight bulge in my sleeve. I have been so lost in thought and distracted by ghostly apparitions that it went unnoticed. It crinkles, is dry and rasps on the fabric inside my jacket. I reach in and tug the item free.

Once more I find paper where I do not expect to find it. It is a small folded note, signed from Oddly. His handwriting is scrawled and barely legible. I stare at it, trying to decode the pen strokes. I cannot decipher his handwriting, and so fold it up and tuck it in my inside pocket for later examination.

The clever boy must have slipped it into my sleeve during our encounter. I thought running into him was chance. Perhaps not.

Before I know what I'm doing, I have dragged my sorry carcass onto a tram and bought a ticket to the wide tree-lined streets of Didsbury, where I march up to the front door of Edgar's town house. I take hold of the large brass knocker, and lift it.

The early afternoon sun is warm in the small pools in which it collects between shadows. These fragmentary splashes of heat do nothing to assuage the pervasive and numbing cold. My breath mists in the air.

The bag on my back is full of the belongings left behind by the Dear Departed. His clothes, his toiletries, his books, his pornography, his photographs, and his hidden letters.

In a moment of clarity it had dawned upon me that the best course of action was to return only *select* belongings to his family. This requires me to do two things.

One; decide exactly which items were appropriate to return. Two; discover the best way in which they should be returned. Additional to these tasks was the deciphering of Oddly's note. But that can wait.

I am unable to simply knock on the DeVeire front door and wish them condolences. The family lives and socialises in very tight exclusive circles. I am sure that if you travel around them too fast you would get terribly dizzy.

Given the reception we received at the funeral, some tact and cunning will be required in order to gain access to their Great House, and to be granted an audience with Beloved Mother.

This is why I am at Edgar's front door, about to knock the pear-shaped brass lump in my hand onto the varnished wood below.

Edgar hails from a family of equal social standing as the DeVeires, and his tall three-storey, double fronted townhouse radiates brash masculine tastes in wide and solid architectural styles, to those who know about such things.

Personally I find it a big show; 'all fur coat and pearls, but no knickers' as my mother would have said. It is an apt description for this imposing terraced building, as once you find yourself across the threshold, it is a very different animal indeed.

I knock once. The sound is a dull thud, and quieter than you might imagine it would be. For a minute I wait, rubbing my hands together to keep them from shivering in the cold. I forgot to wear my gloves again.

The door eventually is opened by a woman of advancing years in something resembling a maid's uniform. It is a deception of course, much like the grand facade of the house.

She smiles at me, and holds her arms out for an embrace. I allow myself to be swept inside. Her skin is olive, and her hair and eyes such a dark brown as to be almost black. When she speaks it is with a very slight accent, but I can not ever place where it is from, as it has been substantially Anglicised by time. She removes the Maid's piny and hangs it upon a hook by the door. It is for appearances only. They do not wish for Edgar to be taken as anything but the lifelong bachelor he purports to be.

Saffron; Edgar's One True Love, links arms with me as we walk through the entrance hall toward the Library. The entrance hall shows the decorative taste of a different nature to the exterior. It is a delicate gleaming box, with expensive portraits of men and women from classic literature on the walls. From the ceiling hangs a wide chandelier, looking for all the world like an exploded snowball, frozen and gleaming, a million tiny precious snowflakes.

"Have you come to stay with us?" She says, looking at the bag on my back.

I say that despite appearances, she is incorrect, "This bag is not full of *my* belongings."

The tinny sound of a distant record player makes its way to my ears. The tune is upbeat, an audible landscape of smooth brass and soft drums.

"It is so sad." Saffron says, patting my hand, the lace of her sleeve brushing my fingertips.

I look at her sideways-on and take her hand in mine. I squeeze it gently.

"He has not been himself." Pitching her voice low, it is obvious that she does not want Edgar to hear her.

"How so?" I ask.

"He does not like to show others he is weak. He believes that to bury his sorrow is the only way a man should grieve. I tell him it is not so. He does not listen. Maybe you can speak with him?"

I notice a small wooden plaque mounted on the wall. Upon it are two coats of arms. One is associated with Edgar's surname. The other must be Saffron's. The quote beneath catches my eye.

Tantum alii, quid vis videre.

'Only let others see what you want them to see'.

I do not know what good my talking to him will do, and I say as much to Saffron, "Edgar only listens to his own council."

"He listens to you." She taps me on the nose, and pushes the door open, announcing; "Edgar, darling, we have a visitor."

The library is one of the rooms off limits to anyone other than close friends. The walls alternate between tall bookshelves and large gilt-framed paintings. The books are arranged to Edgar's own system, which is found to be a bafflement to most other people. The paintings are all of emotive women in states of undress, demonstrating particular fondness for other semi naked women.

Aside from these paintings the decoration is sparse, and there is a fire burning limply in a small hearth. The record player sits on a table in front of the window, flanked by large colourful Tiffany lamps. In the centre of the room a circle of four high-backed leather armchairs face one another. Sitting slouched in one of these chairs, with his feet up on the one opposite is Edgar.

Upon seeing me he sits upright, straightening out his smoking jacket. In his left hand is an open book, and resting on the arm of the chair is a tumbler of what I assume is whiskey. The air is thick, and a layer of cigar smoke hangs at head height. The breeze created by the opening of the door ripples across the room, causing a small grey tide to wash one way, and then the other.

"Rowan." Edgar gestures for me to sit in the chair

recently occupied by his feet, "Didn't expect to see you again today."

Saffron nudges me in the back, and makes a distinctive 'talk to him' gesture with her dark eyes. I nod, and move into the ocean of cigar smog. The door closes quietly, and Saffron has gone.

Edgar's eyes are red. Whether this is from tears, or from the stinging smoke I can not guess. Piled on the seats between us are several books. They all appear to be books of poetry.

"Cigar? Whisky?" Edgar offers.

I shake my head, "No, thank you."

I remove the bag from my back and sit in the free chair opposite Edgar. He watches me, and I can see he is curious about the bag.

"Do you believe in ghosts?" I ask.

His one arched eyebrow raises impossibly further, and he cocks his head to one side, "I can't fathom if you're being serious or not." He says after a short consideration.

"Neither can I." I mutter.

"Have a drink," Edgar encourages, "It'll help."

The record goes quiet between tracks, leaving the hiss and crackle of the needle on the rotating disc to fill the air.

"No, thank you. I had enough at Nell's."

Edgar shrugs, before reaching to the bottle stashed on the floor beside him, and topping up his glass. The bottle is half drained already, yet Edgar shows little sign of being drunk.

"You drank all that this morning?"

He laughs at me, "I'm not that much of a fish. I'll admit that this golden nectar has helped me calm my heart, but I don't need that much of it for the job. This is only my second measure since coming home."

"Saffron's worried about you."

He rolls his eyes, "She thinks I should be more at home with my emotions."

"And what do you think?"

"I am at home with them!" He gestures around the room and at the books on the shelves and the chairs, "They're all around me."

"Those are other people's, not your own."

"Second hand will do me."

He laughs heartily, the sound rattling in his throat, becoming a hoarse cough. I wait patiently as he settles his chest. He catches my eye and wags a finger at me, "Don't you go on at me any more. I've gone near fifty years just fine, without giving in to weeping and wailing."

"That's not what I'm saying. I doubt that's what Saffron is saying."

He harrumphs at me, gulping at his whisky.

"Just allow yourself to feel, without being ashamed of it. Don't be a stranger to yourself." It is a conversation that I have been encouraged to have with him on several occasions in the past. Each time it has been at Saffron's behest, and each time it has ended with Edgar saying the same thing;

"Enough of this silly chatter!"

I sit back in the chair, and cross my left leg over my right, the crook of one knee resting on the bony nobble of its twin, "You didn't answer my question." I say to him, tapping the arms of the chair with my fingertips, "Do you believe in ghosts?"

"Do you?"

"I didn't."

"But something changed?"

"Something changed."

"When?"

"Today."

"At the funeral?"

"At home."

Edgar leans forward, his eyes twinkling with interest. "Tell me everything!"

I shake my head, "Not until you answer my question. Do you believe in ghosts?"

Edgar chuckles at me.

"Would I be this intrigued if I didn't?"

"So that's a yes?"

"Yes."

"Why?"

Edgar is taken aback by my question, and blinks at me slowly. His lively face tweaks up around the cheeks, and he puts his forefinger to his lips, "You tell me your story, and I will tell you mine."

CHAPTER THREE

JUSTICE

He reads me poetry, loudly.

It is by an ancient greek woman whose name I forget, and I'm sure it would be beautiful, if not for the gruff square man reading it in his cigar-raked voice. Or for the record of American Jazz that has finished playing, and is now spinning into hissing oblivion.

Edgar is striding around the small island of chairs, keeping his eyes on the book in his left hand, puffing occasionally on the cigar in his right. I am unsure how I allowed him to begin bellowing these verses at me, but I am regretting it.

I find myself reluctant to tell Edgar how I came to have two visions of the Dear Departed, and the strange conversation we had. It seems so silly, and so vague, like it happened to someone else.

"Today is getting stranger and stranger." I say accidentally aloud.

Edgar stumbles over his words, and over-eggs clearing his throat, before turning his attention once more to the page of the small paperback in his hand.

"Edgar, please," I project into the pause, "May I have a drink after all?"

He grins at me, "Good man."

He produces a second glass from the table below the record player, and pours me a healthy measure. While there, he gently lifts the needle from the record, and flips the disc to play its second side.

"That's quite a lot." I say, looking at the measure in the glass poured for me.

"Seems to me you need it." Edgar winks.

"If you say so."

I sip the single malt, and appreciate how smooth it is. When you spend much of your time languishing at Nell's Place, sampling her various successes and failures at gin-making on the cheap, everything else becomes a joy to consume.

"Sit down," I say to him, "Walking round and round like that, you're making me dizzy."

He does so, puffing a large cloud of foul grey smoke into the space between us.

Following a number of small fuzzy pops the music starts; A smooth driving piano and drum piece, over which a deep female voice swoops and glides.

"Such remarkable things." Edgar nods at the record player, "Music and voices, captured forever. We are all so fleeting on this Earth, we are able to play a record, and hear again the voices of the deceased. Gone but not forgotten."

"Much like a ghost." I say.

He nods slowly, "Yes, after a fashion." His eyes twinkle at me as he squirms, easing his wide bottom into the cushioning of his high-backed chair, "I'm sitting comfortably, young chap. You may begin." He says.

"This morning I thought I caught sight of the Dear

Departed in the window of our room."

Edgar rubs his chin, staring at me, "Could it have been a trick of the light? Some strange distorted reflection?"

"No. He waved at me. And I waved back."

I tell Edgar of the strange feeling it gave me to see him, and how I had found the room to be quite empty when I returned. I expect to be laughed at, or at least made to feel a bit of a fool for my flights of fancy, but Edgar takes me seriously. His focus not once wavering. He is enthralled by my story. I grow more confident in telling it as I continue, as Edgar's honest face encourages me to relax. I finish with the last words he uttered to me before vanishing.

Edgar is now leaning forward, his elbows resting on his knees, listening avidly, "That's it? Is there no more?" He asks.

"And then I gathered his belongings and came here."

He sits back, a thoughtful look on his craggy face, alternating between puffing on his cigar and sipping his drink. Eventually he shakes his head, looking sadly at me.

"I fear, my dear friend, that you are not in your right mind." He says.

From his wrapped attention during my retelling of the visions, I assumed Edgar believed me. I feel my body deflate, as the tension that has been holding it taut and plump escapes. I am punctured by Edgar's dismissal, "Edgar-" I begin, but he cuts me off.

"Rowan, I believe the supernatural flavours our lives with the odd bump in the night. I simply can't believe the

42

dead come strolling around chatting to us, handing out portents of doom or suchlike. It's preposterous!"

I sag further, shrinking into the large chair, "It was so real..." I stare at the glass of whisky clutched in my hands. I am rotating it back and forth, feeling the texture of the cut glass leaving minute impressions upon the skin of my palms.

"In times of grief the mind can play tricks on a person." Edgar's gruff voice is quiet, he reaches forward and pats me on the knee, "Cheer up. You'll be feeling like the bee's knees in no time. Just need to shake off this maudlin grump."

I take a large mouthful of my whisky, swallowing it quickly, and enjoy the spiced pulse of it passing down my gullet.

Edgar's attention moves to my bag, slumped at my feet, "You have those letters with you? The ones you found in the chair?" Curiosity is evident on his animated face. I pull my backpack toward me and slowly open it, pulling out a few items from the top most layers. He takes from me the bundle of hidden letters.

"You've read these?" He asks.

"No. Only one."

"What is this?" He laughs horsely at the doodle of a sickly spaniel. Slowly and carefully he reads another three of the letters, "How very mundane. Tell you what though, there is nothing here to reference any letter from Lawrie to his Beloved Mother."

"How can you tell?" I ask.

Edgar shows me the letters he has read. Each of them contain information leading on from the sagas depicted in the one before.

"It's a one-sided conversation." I say, "He didn't ever write to her?"

"Couldn't have done."

"He didn't ever talk much about his family. What I know of them I prized from him when drunk, or by piecing together clues from his occasional off comments."

Edgar's brow furrows at the bundle of letters, holding one up for me to see, "This is different penmanship." He pulls this letter from its thin envelope and unfolds it.

His eyes flick back and forth along the lines of tiny writing. His brow furrows further, and he tuts, "From that oaf of a brother."

"The man from the funeral?"

"Listen; 'You will bring disgrace to the family. Think of Mother, and think of me.' Angry rambling, angry rambling, 'If you do not return home by this time next month, and give up the filthy life in which you wallow, I shall be forced to drag you home myself'." Edgar flicks through the remaining letters, "There are five from his brother."

After a brief examination of these letters we discover that they become more and more irate as they go on, and once more there is no indication that the Dear Departed ever replied.

"Something occurs to me," I say, finishing my drink, "If Lawrie didn't ever write to his family or respond to these letters, how did either of them know where to write to him, and what 'filth' does the oaf think his brother was wallowing in?"

"I'll leave the filth to your imagination." Edgar winks as me, "As for the other quandary, not a clue." He looks up, a memory fluttering in his eyes, "The two of you were happy as hens." Smiling at me briefly, he goes back to reading the letters in silence.

I rummage through my backpack a little further.

"I need to return his things to his Mother. Well, not everything." I wave the pornographic photographs at Edgar briefly, "I want to return his more personal effects." As I rummage, I realise that something is missing, "Where's his journal?"

"Did you not pack it?" He asks.

I think back. There was nowhere I did not tidy. No stone was left unturned, "I didn't find it. But he wrote in it every day. He never took it out with him. It was always on the writing desk."

"But not today?"

"No."

The fact I did not notice its absence before now is a knife to the gut.

The unlocked door.

My face flushes hot with blood, and I feel a little faint, "Someone *did* break into my room. They must have taken the journal while I was attending the funeral." I feel personally violated at the thought of an uninvited stranger in my room.

I feel dirtied.

Over another glass of whisky Edgar calms my nerves, and to distract me from my spiralling thoughts of intrusion and violation we begin to fathom a way in which I may return the items in my backpack to the DeVeire family.

"A soiree." He says.

"A soiree?" I ask dubiously.

"A soiree!" He cries, "The DeVeire matriarch; a faded Peacock, she's often holding genteel gatherings of select individuals. It truly is an exclusive do."

"So how do I get invited?"

"You don't. I do."

"Oh." I grunt perhaps more childishly than intended.

"And you accompany me as a guest."

"Ah." I sit up taller in my chair.

"Be sure to wear your best suit."

"My best suit?" I look down at myself, "I'm in it."

Having not changed since the funeral, I am still done up very smartly, but not a patch on how polished I would need to look in order to mingle with High Society.

Edgar looks me up and down, tutting, "That won't do at all. I'll ask Saffron to show you up to our wardrobe. You can wear one of mine."

I gently point out that Edgar is in possession of many more inches around the waist than myself, and he laughs at me. It is one of his guttural chortles that collapses into a coughing fit.

"I was once a similar shape to you, and I still have a couple of old suits stashed away. Trust me, we'll dress you properly for the occasion."

As if my belly were full of thunder, my stomach rumbles loudly. I check the time on my wristwatch. Today has flown by. It is nearing half past four in the afternoon, and not one single piece of solid food has passed my lips today.

"Ah perfection!" Edgar beams as Saffron enters the library. She glides forward, pushing a silver trolley before her.

The ornamented little contrivance is covered with plates of cheese, cold cuts of meat, sliced tomatoes with garlic and bread.

"I'm ravenous." Edgar grins.

"Saffron, you are an angel." I thank her as I eye up the food hungrily.

Edgar removes the books from another of the armchairs, and Saffron sits in it, the food on its trolley positioned in the centre of our small island.

"Do not wait to be polite. Enjoy!" She waves a hand at the food.

I don't need to be told twice. I fill a plate with a little of everything, and sit back to devour the kind offering. I watch the two lovers as they sit and eat quietly. Theirs is a subtle and strange body language; loving and warm, yet distant. They have been together since they were both young, when Saffron was employed to be Edgar's Nanny. She is only five years older than him, but he looks much the elder of the pair.

Their love has always been a secret due to Saffron's lower social standing. Edgar's expansive and mighty family would not tolerate any more scandal than the one that had given rise to Edgar in the first place. The two of them look at each other with an intensity and mischief which I hope to someday share with someone.

Alas my life has been predominantly a solitary one, until the Dear Departed came into my life. We became firm friends as fast as a snap of the fingers, and for a short time we were lovers. Though I very much got the impression that it was simply a bit of fun to him. I was a friend who would occasionally get naked with him, and touch him in ways that would make a whore blush. After a tryst we would always retire to our own separate beds, and it would be as if nothing happened when we rose the next morning.

I chew slowly on a slice of cold beef, lost in lurid thoughts of those frisky nights, the way his body would glisten in the dim light, the heat of his breath on the back of my neck, and the deep rhythm of our lust. I am brought back to reality by Edgar clearing his throat.

"Sorry?" I ask, "I was thinking."

"I asked if you'd like a top up?"

I shake my head, and mutter something about needing to get home. It is already dark outside. The winter nights are cold and bitter, and I do not look forward to shivering all the way back to my room.

"No no no. You will sleep here." Saffron is quite adamant, "I have made up the spare room for you."

She is as stubborn as Edgar can be, and to refuse would be impossible. I thank her gently, and fill my plate for a second time.

"You never did tell me your ghost story. I told you mine, now you tell me yours."

"*Dios mio*, not again." Saffron sighs. It is clearly a story she has heard him tell many times before.

"Every time he tells that story, it becomes more phantasmagorical." She says as she leads me to their spare room. Edgar is still in the Library, selecting other records to play while he makes a good start on a second bottle of whisky.

"Edgar doesn't really see a ghost does he?" I ask cautiously.

Saffron replies without looking at me, "Every time he looks in a mirror. His ghost story is a fantasy. He is haunted only by the death of his sibling. He was very young when it happened, and the shadow of it looms large upon him still."

I understand, so will push no further on the subject.

We reach the spare bedroom, and Saffron shows me inside. The curtains are open, permitting a square of moonlight to pool upon the large rug that takes up much of the floor. The bakelite light switch is stiff under my fingers, but when it clicks into position, the wall-mounted lamps warm instantly. They cast their yellowish light into the room, and over its blue papered walls. There is a small fire in the hearth, burning down to glittering embers. I can smell the old wood used as kindling and I find it a welcome change to the smog from the library. Saffron takes a small log from a basket by the fireplace, lodging in amongst the hot ash.

"This will help to keep you warm in the night, and send you to sleep content."

The missing journal is still playing on my mind, and I suspect that sleep will be a stranger to me.

"Stay with us as long as you need." She squeezes my hand kindly, before backing out of the room and closing the door behind her.

I have none of my night clothes with me, and fear that sleeping nude might leave me too cold to be comfortable. Moving to the bed, I run a hand over the soft sheets. A long night shirt has been left folded on the pillow for me. Saffron thinks of everything. Prodding the log in the fire, I will it to catch faster. I am not entirely warm, and want to be before getting undressed. The log basket contains another three solid chunks of lumber. One of these I select, and fit it in with the other in the fireplace. Soon both are popping and crackling, slowly catching light. Small yellow flames dance up from the ash, performing a silent ballet. I sit on the floor, cross legged, staring into the firelight. The heat caresses my face and chest. My eyelids are heavy, and I realise I am much more tired than I thought.

Warmed by the fire and Edgar's whisky, I slip out of my suit and into the nightshirt. I switch off the lights, draw the curtains, and into the plush bed I climb, slowly and carefully, as I feel that to wrinkle and mess the neatly made sheets would be an insult to the woman who made it up for me.

It is a marked difference to my own nest. My bed is narrow, the mattress is thin and lumpy, laid over wooden slats in a cheap frame. My sheets are old and stained, threadbare in places and second-hand. Sometimes I think they smell like someone died in them.

This bed is a palace in comparison! The mattress is well-sprung, and bounces a little under me. The duvet is thick, and the sheets are heavy and soft. There is an abundance of pillows, and my head falls back into them as it would into a cloud. I murmur like a cat purring.

Despite the comfort of my body; laying still and coddled, my mind is writhing like a serpent on hot coals. I feel useless and empty. There is a dull emptiness in my heart. The loss of the Dear Departed still hurts deeply, and the healing has been done no favours by my mind manifesting him as a ghost twice in one day.

As I stare at the ceiling, listening to the sound of distant jazz from Edgar's record player I make a decision. The murder of my friend must be resolved. His murderer must be put to justice. In the morning I would pay a visit to the Rozzers, and inform them of the stolen journal. I am not sure what good it will do to tell them, but every clue they have will enable them to move in on whosoever ended poor Lawrie's life.

"This is a bit posh." says the Dear Departed.

I look over at him, laid next to me. His hands are knotted behind his head, his eyes are closed, and he is smiling. As if I am a violin mid concerto, the sight of the Dear Departed plucks at the taut strings in my chest. I make a strange strangled sound. It is half a sob, and half a laugh.

"There's more of gravy than of grave about you." I quote Dickens, trying to anchor my thoughts in something real, willing my brain to give up this fantasy.

I turn onto my side to see him better. I examine every detail of his angular face.

There is the ridge of faint freckles that form a band across his cheeks and nose. His long eyelashes and his short, wispy sideburns. I trace the strong angle of his jaw, and the high rise of his forehead to his wavy hair, somehow always on the neat side of wild.

"I miss you so much." I say.

"I know."

"Why are you haunting me?" I ask, tentatively reaching a hand toward him.

He opens his eyes and tilts his face sideways to me. His big eyes pucker at the corners as his smile widens.

"Someone has to look after you."

I do not know how long he will linger, and I must ask him some important questions. I need to truly understand if he is a fact or a fiction from my mind. I gulp, and ask him;

"Lawrence, who killed you?"

He shushes me, and takes hold of my outstretched hand. I feel nothing but a strange chill on my fingers. I wonder if I were to move, would my hand pass through his?

"Go to sleep, Rowan. You need to rest. You're safe here for now."

"Aren't I safe at home?"

"You aren't *really* safe anywhere."

"Why?"

In the blink of an eye the Dear Departed is gone.

There is no ripple of spectral light, there is no fading. He is simply vanished, as if he were never there.

"Lawrence?" I sit up and look around the room. The fire glows happily in the hearth, and faint jazz continues to flow through the house. The Dear Departed has departed once more.

I lay back into the plush bedding. I loved Lawrence, and without him I am lost. Damn my brain and heart for not permitting me rest! I need to sleep, and so attempt to focus on the quiet music downstairs. The rise and fall of the dusky vocals like a ship at sea, cresting waves and drifting with the deep currents of brass and piano accompaniment, matching my own sense of having slipped my mooring; adrift.

I do not remember how long it took me to fall asleep but the next time I open my eyes there is bright light daring to peek into the room around the curtains. I feel I have only closed my eyes for a few minutes, but clearly that is the illusion of a dreamless sleep. I stretch my arms and legs, yawning. I wiggle my toes and crack my knuckles. A beautiful smell reaches my nose, and I rise from the comfortable bed eagerly. Bacon and sausages!

I wash and dress swiftly before following the smell of breakfast through the house to the kitchen. I poke my head through the door and discover Saffron and Edgar mid-kiss. I cough politely, and they break apart.

"Don't stop on my account." I chuckle.

Saffron shoos the two of us from the room as she continues to cook.

I make my way to the dining room, where the table has already been laid. This room is adorned with paintings of vividly coloured flowers and wild green places. It is soothingly floral in scent as well, as if the very brush strokes give off the sweet aroma of wild summer roses.

I have awoken in a much better mood than the one in which I fell asleep, and it is helped further when Saffron arrives and deposits a plate in front of me. Eggs, buttered bread, bacon, sausages and black pudding. Delicious. Saffron leaves briefly to fetch her own and Edgar's breakfasts.

My resolve has not altered, and I begin to plan my journey back into the centre of Manchester to visit the Police Station on Newton Street. I tell Saffron of my intentions.

"I hope it will do some good." She says, sitting down to eat her own breakfast of poached eggs and toast.

The joy of a hearty breakfast is dampened by Edgar entering the dining room like a storm cloud, handing me the morning's Newspaper, tapping at a story. Saffron indicates a large teapot with her fork.

"Help yourself."

"Thank you, I will." I say, wiping my lips on an embroidered napkin.

Pushing away my plate, I lay the Newspaper out flat on the table, running my finger along the small lines of text as I read.

MURDER CASE CLOSED

"They think it's just a robbery gone awry?" I ask incredulously.

Edgar nods, pouring himself a cup of tea, "No further lines of enquiry. That's what they say. Reached a dead end, pardon the expression, so the investigation's put its hooves up."

I stutter in angry disbelief, "For the murder of anyone from a family like the DeVeires, they usually don't rest until they've dragged a sorry someone to hang!"

"It's the circumstances. It's where he was found. It's the *connotations*."

"How do you mean?" I am suspicious that Edgar knows something I do not.

He sighs, staring down at his food sullenly, "Lawrie was a dilly boy. Working the streets, making money from men who like to knock knees with other men. The family won't want that scandal, so it's quietly going to go away." He adds a dash of milk to his tea and sips it loudly.

I had known Lawrie was making money somehow, of course, but until that moment I had not realised exactly how he had made it. I assumed he had an inheritance or family fund he was able to access. While I made my money from semi-regularly tending the bar at Nell's Place, he must have been out making money on the streets.

"I didn't know that." My voice is small, and I feel very stupid, "How do you know that?"

Edgar spins his tea cup distractedly, "We wanted to spare you some heartache."

"We?"

"Nell and I." Edgar says.

"You both knew?"

"Only what the Whisperers told Nell."

Those damned Whisperers!

Lady Nell maintains that they are the most efficient way of spreading information around the city without the authorities hearing it.

I think they're a bunch of gossip-hungry ragamuffins who will do anything to make a quick bit of money or cause a small sensation for whoever is on their personal hit list that week. Temperamental, unreliable, but vital. It had been this chain of informants that had first alerted us to the demise of dear Lawrence. Without them we would know nothing of his passing, when his funeral had been, or where.

"Those blasted Whisperers."

Edgar nods, "I know."

Saffron pours me some tea, adds milk and sugar, then pushes it into my hand, "He is going to the Police." She says across the table to Edgar.

There is a sudden alarm in his eyes, and his jowls stiffen. He looks at me, his one permanently raised eyebrow dipping briefly into a scowl with its counterpart.

"Why?" He asks.

"I'm going to tell them about the intruder and the stolen journal."

Edgar snatches up the newspaper and waves it at me, "Case *closed*, it says here. It'll do no good. I know what they're like. It will only bring trouble to our doorsteps, mark my words." He folds the paper up and slides it away from us all down the long table.

Saffron tuts at him. Edgar exhales loudly through his nose, stabbing a sausage with his fork. He lifts the whole thing up and takes a big bite off one end, chewing angrily.

"Don't let him bother you with his tantrums, Rowan." Saffron says to me in a stage whisper, "If you believe that it will do some good, go."

"What have I got to lose? If nothing else, I believe it will help me regain perhaps a little of my sanity," I say to Edgar, "Thank you for your hospitality." This second comment I address to Saffron. She smiles and dips her head in gratitude, "If I may, I'll leave Lawrie's things here until we can arrange to meet the DeVeires?"

Edgar nods and Saffron smiles, "Of course. I have already tidied them away into the study." She says.

"In that case," I announce as I rise from the table, "If you'll excuse me, I must be off to ensure that justice prevails."

Neither Edgar or Saffron rise from the table as I leave the dining room, and my ears catch the faintest of murmurs from Edgar, which sounds suspiciously like a reluctantly offered 'good luck'.

I hope his hangover doesn't last too long.

Chapter Four

New Evidence

The tram rattles my bones and nearly shakes my eyes from their sockets on the seemingly endless journey from Didsbury into the centre of the city. I sit on the lower deck, as it is far too cold this time of year to ride in the open-air upper level. Across the isle from me a large woman sits swaddled in a thick fur coat. The legs of whichever unfortunate animal lost its life to fashion dangle below her sagging cheeks, making it appear that her head is attempting to escape her body on thin furry limbs. I suppress a chuckle at the absurd thought.

Seated near the front of the vehicle is a man huffing loudly at the stories of scandal and intrigue in the morning's newspaper. Every now and then he leans to the woman seated beside him and explains why each story offends him so. Everything offends him. I feel sorry for his suffering wife. She has the glazed expression of someone who deliberately stopped listening a long time ago.

Gradually the tram descends into the paved valleys and canyons that run between the high cliff-faces that are the buildings of the city centre. They loom over me, almost menacing, bending over the road to peer at me through their grimy glass paned eyes. The sky rests further away from you in the city, pinned aloft by pointed roofs and robust chimneys perched on red brick facades.

A small knot of apprehension pulls tight in my stomach as I think of my destination. Looking around the carriage once more, the plump and indifferent faces of my fellow passengers seem sallow, their eyes darting in my direction.

Crooked lips pull away from stained teeth, jeering. The elegant painted nails of the ladies are talons and meat hooks, sharpened and eager for my throat. My nerves are playing tricks on me, and I turn my face to the window again.

Today the weather is calm, and here and there the grey clouds part to reveal a glimpse of blue. It is raining lightly. I have my hands firmly clenched in my pockets to keep them warm as I step off the tram into Piccadilly.

The bustle of people sweeps me with it, and my feet match pace with those around me. A place like Piccadilly is where you can see all the layers of society mashed together. The wealthy and the wretched all pass through places like this, giving it a unique and electric atmosphere, even at half nine in the morning, as it is now.

I navigate between people, tripping over my own feet once, and someone else's twice. Newton street is long and wide. On the left I see the Police Station growing larger as I approach. It is a fat building, all squares and sharp angles. It is dark and imposing, with its clustered officers a mere peppering of humanity around the obelisk of the Law. Horses and carts compete with Motorcars for priority and space.

A doubt begins to flit around my brain, like a wasp around jam. Edgar is sure there is no use in presenting Hilda Handcuffs with new evidence. I want justice. The police have never cared much for the likes of me or my friends, but I hope that the men employed in the imposing station must want the same as me in this instance; to find the horrid person who killed Lawrie.

I waft away the stinging doubt and enter the station through the blue front door, over which a decorative iron arm holds a large blue-glass lantern emblazoned with the word Police.

As soon as I am through the door, the wasp of doubt buzzes louder in my ear. Here I stand, in the entrance to a cave of wolves, a tiny bleating lamb. But a defiant lamb. The faces of the officers that pass me are hung, grey and savage. They carry bruises and scars as a visual history of every time someone fought back.

"Excuse me?" I say, approaching a constable. He has a large nose overhanging a wide broom of grey. The moustache twitches up and down as he speaks to me, but at no point can I see his lips.

"Reporting a crime?"

I nod, "Well, sort of."

"Crimes, misdemeanours, sort-of crimes, almost crimes, slight mishaps. We get all sorts reported. Go speak to the Desk Sergeant. Waste his time not mine."

The constable nods over at a high desk behind a wooden partition. At this desk sits a vast old man, round like a ball, and with outstanding white mutton chops.

Police officers are milling here and there, occasionally leading a restrained criminal in from the street, checking them in with the Desk Sergeant, then dragging them off, snarling into the bowls of the building, to be digested by the processes of the law.

I find a break in the traffic to approach the Sergeant.

He does not look up at me, "Yes?"

"Good morning. I believe I have some information that may help one of your investigations."

"That so?"

My nerves are fluttering and I get ahead of myself, stumbling over my words, "Someone broke into our room, you see. They stole his journal."

The old man leans back in his seat, creaking as he does so, "What's this? Which investigation is this connected to, young man?"

I take a deep breath, "Sorry. It's in relation to the murder of Lawrence Clifford DeVeire."

The old man stiffens slightly. He tries to hide the reaction from his face, but his body language changes immediately, "Now you listen to me, turn around, go home. Don't bother yourself with Police matters." His voice is hushed, and carries an unmistakable urgency.

"I have new information for you. Don't you want to catch the killer?"

"It's been dealt with. Now go home." He is firm, but not unkind.

Behind the Sergeant appears an officer of much higher rank. He is sturdy and tall, athletically built under his thick blue wool uniform coat, "What's your name?" The new officer asks.

I catch the eye of the Sergeant, and something in his expression tells me I should have followed his instruction when he said to leave.

"Rowan."

"Rowan?"

"Rowan Forrester."

"Well Rowan Forrester, I am curious to know what you think will be so interesting to us about the tragic demise of young Mr DeVeire."

In for a penny, in for a pound.

I take stock of all that has occurred, and all I feel I might want to spew out in garbled anxious syllables. Taking another long deep breath I focus on the facts. I focus on the things that the Police will need to know, "He lived with me. The day of his funeral someone broke into our room at Mrs Taffeta's lodging house and stole his journal. I believe that whoever stole the journal may also be responsible for his murder."

The Officer nods slowly, his hands clasped behind his back, not saying anything.

"That's it. That's the information." I conclude.

What more does he want?

He's standing there staring at me as if I am still talk-ing, looking me up and down. I don't like the way his narrow eyes slide over my small form, wiping their strange gaze across every inch of me.

"Well?" I ask, feeling more sure of myself now, "Are

you going to stand there like a garden ornament or do something?"

The Officer smiles a vicious toothy grimace. I can't tell if I have amused him or made him angry, whichever it is I don't like the result, "Mr Forrester, thank you so very kindly for this information, but the case is closed."

I shake my head, "It can't remain closed, surely? You need to reopen it and-"

He interrupts me, "Most thefts from communal lodgings such as yours are perpetrated by someone from within the house. Often the Landlord. Go home. This information is of no value to us."

I open my mouth to argue, but think better of it. The Desk Sergeant indicates the door, "Go on, lad. On your way."

Why did I expect anything different? Edgar knew, and he was right. I thank them both for their time.

Several Constables turn their canine snouts in my direction as I leave, taking in my scent and sizing me up. The Officer turns and wanders away, not caring to watch me leave. His uniformed hounds then become equally dismissive of me, turning away to continue with their own business.

I feel a fool to have ever considered turning to the Police for help. That was that. The Dear Departed will not see justice.

As I walk away from the Station, my head is bowed and my hands are clenched in my pockets. Looking down at myself, I realise how uncomfortable I am in yesterday's clothes, and how scruffy I must look in a wrinkled shirt and trousers. No wonder the Police didn't take me seriously.

I turn onto Stevenson's Square, then begin to navigate my way through a series of side streets until I find myself back at my own home. My feet are very good at finding their way. I put in the minimal effort to drive them forward, one after the other, and they usually guide me safely, even from the most obscure corners of these tangled streets. Today they ache from being stuffed into my smart shoes for far too long. I am eager to put myself into some more comfortable clothes and my old shoes. They are worn in just the right places that make the leather soft to the touch, and easy on the toes.

Mrs Taffeta collars me on the way in. She has the hearing of a hawk, and always seems to lurk near the doorway, ready to pounce and deliver another awkward conversation full of gossip about people I don't know.

"That Tiffin has been up all night *howling* again." She says, striking a match to light her cigarette.

I don't care what the other occupants of the house get up to, so long as they don't disturb me. Being in the roof of the building means that I very rarely get disturbed.

"Mrs Taffeta, I asked you yesterday if anyone had been in my room."

Her face lights up at the prospect of an actual conversation. I get the impression that everyone else in the house avoids her as much as I do. She takes a long drag on her cigarette before replying, the red embers pulling swiftly up the white shaft towards her fingers.

"Was that yesterday? I lose track of days so easily. I only know when Monday is because the milkman comes around and tells me so." She flicks the end of her cigarette with her thumb nail, setting free a shower of ash.

"While I was out at Lawrie's funeral someone broke into our room. They stole his journal. Please think, did you let anyone in?"

"His journal? Why would someone steal a journal? Was there some salacious gossip in there?"

I roll my eyes, "Given that it has been stolen, very probably. That might be why it was stolen. Did you let anyone in?"

She takes another long drag on the cigarette, leaving faint lipstick smears on an end crushed flat by her pinched mouth, "I did not let anyone in." She says, "Well, that's what he told me to say anyhow."

"Who?"

"The man who I didn't let in. Oh wait. No." Cursing herself, she shuffles her slippered feet away from me as fast as she can.

"Wait, Mrs Taffeta!" For an old lady she can shuffle at great speed. Her parlour door slams shut in my face, and I hear the lock click.

I bang on the door. Whoever this mystery man was, it alarms me that my LandLady has lied to me, and allowed him into our room.

"Mrs Taffeta open the door. Who did you let in?"

"No one."

"Fine. Who didn't you let in?" I try my luck, but I know I won't get a helpful answer.

"No one."

I bang on the door again. This receives a loud hiss from Mrs Taffeta's old gramophone, as she begins playing a brash military record to drown me out.

I give up banging on the door, and retire in the direction of my room. I mount the protesting stairs. Looking up I see the hole in the roof has still not been fixed, and today instead of a small shower of rain, it lets in a bitter draught. I bow my head and concentrate on not falling through the worn steps.

"Was that you that made her put that racket on?"

I look up in surprise to see a woman peering out of her doorway at me. She is around my age, with acidic blonde bobbed hair and the remains of yesterday's makeup on her face. She is unashamedly standing there in her night clothes.

The sight of her dressed in such a way doesn't bother me one jot, but society deems it unseemly, and so to preserve her modesty I avert my eyes.

"Sorry, yes." I mutter, as I hurry past. A strong aroma seeps from her open door, sickly sweet and not at all pleasant.

"I was up all night, and now I won't get a wink of sleep. I hope you're happy with yourself." She jabs a finger in my direction aggressively, "Tiffin needs her beauty sleep!"

And then she too slams a door in my face.

Until today I had only ever heard her peculiar bathroom utterances. Now I have a face to put to the name and the noises.

My room is as I left it. I pull the curtain over the window to cut out the dim light of the day and strip out of my clothes, leaving them in an untidy pile at my feet before falling onto my bed. It is stiff and unforgiving, but it is comfortingly familiar. It is mine.

I lay on my back, naked as the day I was born as I try to empty my head of all the muddlesome thoughts of the previous day. More than anything else I try and expunge the feeling of the police officers eyes on me, those prickly hot, predatory gazes.

I cannot lay here and rest. I still feel that justice must prevail. I am full of an energy that must not be squandered and so I pull myself off of my bed and quickly around my room to freshen up and to slide into my more comfortable clothes. Corduroy trousers in a dark mustard, loose cotton shirt, with a blazer in a shade of yellow which almost matches my trousers.

I pin to my lapel a sprig of lavender. I wear it cautiously, but with a small sense of pride. This delicately unobtrusive flower will indicate to those in the know that I am one of them. A secret code. A small symbol of the hidden world beside the everyday humdrum life of the city of which I am a part.

If the Police are intent on allowing justice to go

wanting, I have an idea of how I can begin my own investigation.

I hurry from my room, from the building, and across the city to a small road off Sackville Street, to Nell's Place.

The posies have been replaced, and their fresh smell is a welcome change to the sour stink of the nearby canal, but they do not completely hide it.

Nell is alone in her private room behind the bar. It is a bedroom, kitchen, bathroom and storeroom all in one. Her bed is a pile of cushions on a mattress on the floor. A bath stands against one wall, full of something which might eventually be gin, and the rest of the space is littered with boxes and abandoned clothes. In one corner is a small gas stove, atop which sits a rusty kettle. The walls are hidden by mismatched curtains nailed to the rafters, and by an assortment of large mirrors, some of which are clean.

She is perching daintily on the side of the bath, swirling one painted fingernail in a figure of eight across the liquid's surface, "Thirsty?" She asks.

"Yes, thank you." I nod.

She reaches for a small glass, dips it into the bath and holds it out to me, her little pinky pointed daintily in the air.

"A cup of tea would do me." I say.

She shrugs, sipping the gin herself. Pulling a grimace, she chokes the words; "Probably for the best."

The bruise on her face has lessened a shade, but in its centre is still a deep plum. She is dressed in a simple dark knee length dress, wrapped loosely in a silk dressing gown which has seen better days. She isn't wearing any stockings and so her willowy legs like those of an ivory doll are on display.

"What brings you round looking so full of beans?" She asks, rising from her languid pose on the rim of the tub. I often forget how remarkably tall she is. If she stands close to me I can see right up her nose.

"Justice."

"Justice?"

"And information."

"Now *that* I can provide."

We move into the front of Nell's Place, and find somewhere comfortable to sit. Before too long the kettle is whistling, and a pot of tea is provided. I fill Nell in briefly on my visit to the Police, during which she sits quietly, looking off at some distant intangible nothing, listening to me intently.

I decide to omit any mention of what may or may not be the ghost of the Dear Departed. I don't want to have to go through that conversation again.

When I finish, she turns her large pale eyes to me.

"You think you can be judge and jury to the monster who took Lawrie from us?"

Her reaction takes me by surprise. I had expected her to be on board in an instant. It seems that she may need a little convincing.

"I just want to find out who it was. Then Hilda

Handcuffs can do what they're good at."

Nell shakes her head, "Sure as eggs, you're taking three steps forward before thinking of the first. That's a way to trip over yourself for certain."

"I'm not." I scoff, sounding like a petulant child.

She smiles at me, "No?"

"No."

From the pot I pour myself a cup of slightly brown water. It must be tight around here at the moment. She's reusing tea leaves again.

"The Rozzers didn't care earlier today. Why should they care tomorrow, or the day after, or whenever you have the information you want?"

"It'll be evidence. Something that can't be ignored. And if they don't listen, well, maybe I'll go to the papers."

She looks at me for a long time, those pale eyes of hers boring into me like dentist drills.

"I'm sure the Evening News would love to run a bit of juicy scandal." I wink at her.

At the mention of her favourite word she allows herself a little smile, scratching the side of her equine neck with those vivid nails.

I forge on; "The Whisperers. That chain of informants across the city, they were the ones who told you. Before anyone else knew who it was that had been killed. Before the Police or the papers."

She nods slowly.

"So," I continue, "which of them told you? Which of

71

them told them? And them? And so on?"

A light of comprehension dawns on her heart shaped face, "Fancying yourself a preternatural Holmes? You want to track the information to its source?"

"I do. If they knew it was Lawrence, and knew where, and when, one of them must have been there when it happened. One of them must have seen who did it." I am leaning forward in my seat now, keen for Nell to be on board with my plan. I'd need her and her connections to follow this through, but she hesitates.

"The Whisperers come to me because I can be trusted to keep schtum about where the gossip comes from. 'Nell' means to listen, and that's what I do. That's all I do."

I reach out and take one of her hands in mine.

"Please, for me. You know I can be trusted. But more than that, for Lawrie. For his memory."

"And for your peace of mind?"

"For my sanity."

Reluctantly she agrees. But makes me swear an oath to never reveal the identity of any of the people I would meet.

I swear it.

We finish the pot of tea and set off.

CHAPTER FIVE

WHAT THE WHISPERERS HEARD

Our first stop is at the residence and practice of one Doctor T Mandelbaum. A maid shows us to a room in which we must wait to be seen. She eyes us up curiously as we sit in the uncomfortable wooden chairs that face the small fireplace. There are two others waiting in this room, a nervous young lady and a woman of innumerable years and impressive girth.

Lady Nell is wearing her large dark glasses once again, to hide her black eye. The dim light in the room and the glasses render her almost blind, and in finding her chair she almost fell over it.

"Why don't you take off the glasses?" I ask, with a respectful hush. Heaven forbid I should disturb the other occupants of the room.

"Fish and chips to that!" Nell says dismissively, somewhat louder than necessary.

The two women sitting quietly nearby try very hard to look at anything they can that isn't us.

"I hope the good Doctor has a cure for me." Nell's voice becomes slightly louder still. She isn't shouting, but it fills the room, cutting the still air into pieces, "I fear I am terribly contagious."

She over-acts a cough in the direction of the young lady, who visibly flinches, and then another at the older lady, who scowls deeply, "So very terribly horribly contagious."

She hides a smirk with her hand, then once more she coughs at the two women.

The younger of the two scurries from the room, head bowed. We hear the maid protesting her sudden exit, but is cut short by the front door slamming shut. Nell stares at the remaining woman.

"What are you looking at?" The chins of the woman wobble giddily as she clucks.

Lady Nell shrugs, pretending to nibble one fingernail, "Just wondering if you've anything of value worth stealing amongst your various geographic regions." With her free hand, she vaguely indicates the woman's body.

Affronted, the large lady shifts the mountain ranges of her form and goes the way of the younger woman a few moments before.

"What was that all about?" I ask.

"Can't have anyone earwigging on our conversation. Plus I can't be chuffed waiting."

A few minutes of silence elapse, both of us comfortable in our quiet company. Eventually I ask her how she came by her black eye.

"Oh just some butch ducky who didn't take too kindly to me in the cottage."

I understand her coded speech, and decide to leave any more questions until we are in private. At that moment someone steps into the room. He is a plain middle aged man with a receding hairline. His clothes are smart but drab. His pale face drops when he sees Nell, and his watery eyes show a flicker of fear at the flower in my lapel.

"*Oy vey.*" He says, shoulders sagging.

Nell grins at him, "Hello Doctor. I have a problem that I hope you can help me with."

He gestures limply for us to follow him, and we do.

His consultation room is dark and smells of leather and medicinal alcohol, and reverentially Dr Mandelbaum takes his seat behind the wide desk. His chair is positioned in front of the tall window, casting him as a squat dark shape before the bright oblong. On the walls hang disturbing anatomical illustrations, and a skull sits on the mantelpiece, its hollow eyes looking out of the window.

I take a seat opposite the Doctor, expecting Nell to take up the one next to mine. Instead, she drifts around the room, examining the various illustrations and knick-knacks that attract her magpie attention.

The Doctor is swamped by his enormous desk, and looks to be uncomfortable in his chair.

"What can I do for you?" He asks, addressing Nell.

He seems to be doing a very fine job of pretending I'm not here. Nell doesn't respond, instead she nods her head from me to him. It seems I am to do the talking.

"Hello Doctor Mandelbaum." I start.

He closes his eyes in frustration. Clearly Nell's presence alarms him, but mine is somehow worse. I continue to speak to the little man, sat there with his eyes screwed up tight, as if the very sound of my voice causes him an earache.

"I am in need of a name. I am looking to trace the

Whisperer who first alerted us to the death of Lawrence De-Veire."

At the mention of the Whisperers the small Doctor flinches, and his hands fly to his face, rubbing his eyes.

"Please, I need your help."

A whimpering laugh leaps involuntarily from Mandelbaum's mouth. It is the sound of barely controlled panic.

His distress confuses me, and I turn to Nell for some guidance. She tuts. Deftly she has tucked some small gilded ornament into her coat pocket.

Her heels click on the wooden floor, and she bends forward, leaning her elbows on the desk, resting her chin on elegantly entwined fingers.

"Sour as vinegar, this one." She says to me, "He's semi-regular at my Place, giving away tidbits of tattle like they're going out of fashion."

"Uh-huh." I say.

"He drinks, he speaks, I listen."

I begin to understand, "And does the good Doctor also give away lots of information about his patients that he perhaps ought not to?"

Blackmail?

I am not too happy about stooping to this devious low, but given the mission we are engaged in, I understand the need for expediency.

Nell nods, "And if he doesn't spill the beans on who told him about the Dear Departed, I might just-"

The small man snaps, standing up rigidly like a pole

has been thrust up the back of his shirt, "You wouldn't dare!"

Nell chuckles, "Oh I'd dare, dear."

I attempt to placate the upset man, "You know what she's like. Loves a scandal."

The Doctor now turns his full attention to me.

"You wear *that* so flagrantly!" He hisses, pointing at the flower in my lapel, "You could bring my Practice into disrepute. Do you know how hard it can be to find decent paying clients? I can't afford the cost of losing any more patients. I'd be destitute."

"Some are bolder than others." Lady Nell says cooly as she turns and sits on the desk, leaning back just enough to break the Doctor's line of sight to me.

I finger the delicate lavender. I wear it so often I forget it's there. It is my signal to others like me that they are safe in my presence, that I am not a threat to them.

Yet in this scenario, outside of my usual haunts and away from my regular routes about the city, it has had the opposite effect. A gulf lays between myself and Mandelbaum's viewpoint. I find solace and comfort in the flower, and he sees danger and risk and the hard underside of a police boot crashing down.

Doctor Mandelbaum's face is slick with sweat. He is scared. Though he is still a shaded shape before the window, my eyes have adjusted to this theatrically back-lit medical practitioner. I reexamine his face. On his collar is the faintest trace of white powder, and his cheeks seem to bare the remains of rouge.

Now I know why he is so scared, "Are you a quean?"

He does not respond, but the flicker of his eyes tells me all I need to know. He is a man who has first hand experience of the underside of a police boot. Possibly more than once.

I am taken back suddenly to my visit to the Police station, and those hungry faces. Eyes flaming hot and ice cold in equal measure, and the slick oily stain they left across my body.

"If I give you a name will you go?" Mandelbaum says, his voice small.

"Not just any old name." Lady Nell wags a finger at the Doctor.

He takes up a pen and a piece of paper. He writes a name and address and hands it to Nell. She looks at it quickly, then folds it and slips it into her pocket.

As we leave, Nell blows the Doctor a kiss.

"He wasn't too happy, was he?" I comment to Nell as we navigate our way from Doctor Mandelbaum's Practice.

"He's married to a very fine woman, but there isn't much mustard in his sandwich. You pegged him, sure as eggs." Nell is striding confidently ahead of me, her long legs carrying her slightly faster than my usual gate. I quickstep to keep up.

"He's a regular at the Balls and at the bathhouses." She continues, "Though you'd never know it's him. Done up like a wedding cake."

"Did you know that Lawrie was working the streets before he was killed?" I ask suddenly.

The question had been bubbling up all morning, and it spills out of my lips unbidden.

Nell stops so quickly that I almost walk into the back of her. She turns and pulls her glasses down their perch, so that she can look me in the eye, "Would it matter if I did?"

I nod, "I don't like the idea that my friends are keeping secrets from me."

Nell rests her hands on my shoulders, "It was not my secret, it was *his*. And it was not my place to tell anyone. Remember, I listen. That's what I do. That is all."

A dim flame of rebellion wells in my gut, "That's so passive! You have this vast network of informal informants across the city. Imagine what you could achieve if you changed how you used them."

"How so?"

"I'm not sure, actually." I admit, and she takes back her hands.

"Thinking two steps ahead without looking at the pit right in front of you, as always. Focus on the business at hand."

I follow in Nell's feline wake to our next destination; a small Tailor's outfitters squeezed into a row of delicatessen shops and wine merchants.

I have lost my bearings entirely, and though we haven't walked too far, I can no longer tell where in the city we are.

Today's variety of rain is light and infrequent, the chill in the air less than recent days, and having forgotten to bring my gloves out with me again, this is a relief.

A small bell sings a polite *dingalingaling* as Nell pushes the door open. She sweeps in, a slow cyclone of cheap perfume and second hand glamour.

"I'd like to speak to Tremblay. Are they in?" This she addresses to a young girl stationed at the counter, whose eyes boggle slightly at our sudden appearance. It has clearly been a very slow day.

From some unseen place, the sound of a sewing machine can be heard at work in short bursts.

"He's workin' in t' back. You need ya fur seein' to?" The girl reaches out to touch Nell's coat, causing the woman to recoil as if from a snake, batting away the advancing fingers.

"I must speak with him in person." Nell says, loudly enough to be heard in the back rooms of the shop. The sound of the sewing machine halts abruptly.

"Show her through." Comes a heavily accented voice from the depths of the room beyond.

Said room is an avalanche of colours, where it is reams of fabric that are cascading downhill rather than snow and ice. In the centre of this slow cave-in sits a man hunched at his juddering machine.

He is tall and bent, thinner even than Lady Nell, yet without the skeletal or malnourished appearance you might expect from someone barely as wide as my thumb.

This is Tremblay, the Whisperer who passed on the information about Lawrie's murder to Mandelbaum.

I feel one large step closer to discovering something vital. The more information I am able to gather, the more sure I am that Justice will be served to whomever deserves it.

The insectoid man lifts his foot from the pedal, and the machine pauses. He looks up slowly with wide, dark eyes. His face is powdered and he wears an obvious white hairpiece. His tailored suit is striped in shades of blue and pink, and his shoes shine brightly with polish.

"*Oui*?" He shrugs at us, holding out his long hands, "I can help you?"

Lady Nell strides around the room, fingering some of the finer swathes of fabric as she passes, "I do hope so." She purrs, "Firstly, you can tell me..." She lifts a swatch of red silk, and wraps it around her neck, slipping in a knot to hold it in place. "...is this my colour?" She asks, posing for us.

I chuckle at her, and she scowls.

"You can just say no."

Tremblay's agile fingers move swiftly to remove the silk from Lady Nell's neck, "I think it is not your colour. Or in your price range, madame."

"Mademoiselle." Lady Nell corrects him.

"*Si tu le dis.*"

As entertaining as it is to watch Nell antagonise yet another strange Whisperer, I hope to get some useful information before the end of the day. She is wasting time with affected campery and her trademark brand of hijinks.

"Mister Tremblay, we know you passed on information regarding the murder of Lawrence DeVeire." I say.

The French tailor growls at me. He actually growls, curling his lip in anger, "I knew that Meddle-barmy could not be trusted." Tutting, he turns to his machine where he begins rethreading his needle with a fresh reel, "So what of it?" he spits.

"We want to know who told you." I remain calm, trying to keep my voice neutral.

His fingers stop their frantic movements, and his head snaps up to catch me in an electric stare, "*Pourquoi*?"

"I want to track the whispers to their source. Someone was there with him when he died. I need to find out who. I need to find out what happened."

Tremblay's expression softens, "You loved the boy?"

I am embarrassed to speak the truth out loud. My awkward silence says enough.

The tailor sits at his machine, leaning back in his chair, crossing his legs and folding his arms, "*Oh l'amour. Je suis très occupé*, but I can spare some small time. However, you will owe me a great favour."

I nod quickly, "Anything."

Lady Nell nudges me, "Never promise to pay *anything*. You're dreadful at this espionage lark. Always maintain the position of mystery and power."

Tremblay snorts, "How you think you have any power is a mystery *pour moi*."

I move forward, eager to hear what the slender man has to say about Lawrie. He looks at me, and there is a glimmer of something in his eye. A kindness, or an understanding.

He smiles a thin smile, and takes one of my hands in both of his, "*Gentil garçon*, you will not enjoy what I say."

"It doesn't matter." I respond quickly.

It doesn't matter one jot how unpleasant it is, I need to hear it. I need to hear something, anything, to get me closer to the truth, and to being able to put my mind and the troublesome phantasm that plagues me to rest.

"I do not know all the information. What I do know; there was an argument. Whoever it was, he knew him. They were familiar with one another. The argument escalated, and poor young DeVeire met his demise on the end of brutal fists."

Tremblay apologises for not knowing more, and offers his condolences. He seems genuine and sincere, and his kindness touches me. The sadness with which he speaks makes me think he too feels this loss.

"Did you know him?" I ask.

"We had crossed paths now and again. *Coquet, beau, gentil.*"

Lady Nell makes a small noise in the back of her throat, the meaning of which is lost on me, but it prompts Tremblay to become slightly defensive, "I would never think to taint such a beauty with my creaking old bones. I admired him from afar. We spoke only now and again."

I press Tremblay on where and when he would see Lawrie out and about. Clearly he had witnessed him working. If he is able to identify the streets and roads on which the Dear Departed picked up clients we find ourselves yet another clue closer to the truth.

Across the room I spy Nell furtively fingering some fine pieces of fabric.

"I do not recall specifics." He shrugs, "Here or there. Always dark, never under the light of lamps."

This nugget of information seems at first mundane, until I recall that only certain streets have electric illumination. Many old gas lamps line the city's pavements and have yet to be replaced, dim as a firefly, or completely defunct.

It is down these shadier streets that many people of our queer twilight demimonde might meet, gather, and converse in the relative safety of penumbra.

The Police prefer the brighter streets, the better to see and be seen in. The tall hat often deterrent enough for the majority of people.

Tremblay passes his dark eyes over me appraisingly.

"You must let me dress you."

"Excuse me?"

Nell claps happily, "Oh yes! Do! He needs a fine suit, sure as eggs!"

Tremblay produces a cloth tape measure from his breast pocket, and with a practiced deftness, runs it up my inside leg. I exclaim in surprise at the sudden proximity of his hands to my underwear, and the items contained therein.

Just as quickly as his hands were there, they are gone, and moved elsewhere. My arms are lifted and various measurements are taken. I have never been measured for a suit before today, and I am sure there were more measurements taken than were needed, and I am sure there was much more laying on of hands around my chest and buttocks than there should have been.

"I'm quite alright for a suit, I think." I back away from the tall Frenchman. I am not averse to such physical contact, but it must be on my terms.

Tremblay shakes a finger, "*Vous êtes débraillé.* You need one of my suits. Which fabrics do you enjoy?"

Lady Nell, at first eager at the thought of me having a suit made for me, is now feeling somewhat ignored. She swoops between the two of us, unravelling a reel of deep brown tweed as she does so, "This, with a blue lining! That will be fine as marmalade! Now, back to business. Who was it told you?" While Tremblay and myself have been speaking, she has managed to slip several swathes of silk into her voluminous coat pockets.

Tremblay tuts at her, moving to roll the tweed up once more, speaking as if to the fabric in his hands, "I was down by the canal with a young labourer. She interrupted us. *Elle a gâché notre soirée.* She often appears unbidden with grotesque information to share. I am sure she is a witch. Her name, I think, is Pasternak."

"Where can we find her?" Nell's pockets are quite full now. Tremblay shrugs, the tweed rolled neatly and put back in its place, he sits at his machine once again.

"*Je ne sais pas.* Go for a walk by the canal. She will find you." His foot begins to rock back and forth on the pedal of his sewing machine, sending the needle into rapid bobbing action, "If you will excuse me. *Je suis très occupé.*"

As we depart I ponder out loud, "What do you think he'll want as a favour in return for what he's told us?"

Lady Nell beams at me. It is the particular smile she uses when being coarse, "Probably wants you to butter his croissant." Laughing at my grimace, she links arms with me, and drags me from the shop.

"To the canal!" she exclaims.

She exclaims it a few more times, as we reach turnings and cross-roads, "To the canal!"

"This way to the canal!"

"To the canal, yonder!"

As I am dragged by Nell's vivid claws, I ponder briefly on who Lawrie's assailant was.

He knew him.

Perhaps it was a previous 'client'.

I can hear the trains pulling into and out of Piccadilly Station when the wind blows the sounds in our direction; deep throbbing and hissing.

A damp mist has begun to descend upon the city. The top-most reaches of the tallest buildings are hazy and hard to make out among the varying shades of grey that hang in the air. Street lamps don't help at all, they simply create an

orb of brightness, where the light bounces off of the minuscule specs of water in the air. This ricocheting of light does
cast an occasional splash of colour in the form of a fragment-
ed rainbow, but they are brief, subtle and ghostly.

We stop at a small bridge over the canal, by the side
of which a worn set of stone stairs lead down to the water's
edge. In one direction the canal is open-topped and bathed
in milky light. In the other it runs under the city, and into
darkness.

"I wonder where we can find the old witch?" I muse.

Nell snorts at me removing her sunglasses and slipping them into a bulging pocket, "There's no such thing as
witches. That old trifle was just trying to give us the heebie
jeebies. She's likely to be some destitute floozy, too long in
the tooth and too saggy of the buttock for paid work on the
streets, so she'll have gone where it's dark and the punters
can't see the merchandise."

"Do you think...?"

Nell shrugs, taking my hand and pulling me gently
but firmly after her down the steps, "I do sometimes."

The noises of the city become muffled and distorted
as we move slowly into the darkness of the tunnelled canal.
The mist has not yet crept across the water's surface, which
ripples and undulates in its rigid bed of brick and mortar.

A sudden movement in a recess makes me jump, and
I clutch hold of Nell. At the dank edge of the tunnel two men
stop what they are doing.

"You're going to get ever such mucky knees." Lady

Nell chirps at one of the men, giggling.

They glare at us.

We continue around a slight bend in the path of the tunnel, and the men are swallowed by darkness.

"You should get yourself down here some day. Getting a slap round the chops from an anonymous saveloy will be good for you." She speaks at a normal volume, yet the closeness of the ceiling, and the mirroring surface of the canal reflect it upon itself, making it seem a great deal louder than it is.

I shush her gently, replying in quieter tones.

"I'm fine thanks."

"You aren't going to find another one like him, you know that?"

"I know."

"You two were made for each other. Such a shame."

I'm not sure how to respond, and so I don't. My ears catch the sound of fabric rustling and wet slapping, and soon enough we pass another couple of young men, this time going at it like rabbits.

"Like to watch?" One of them asks, winking.

Nell pauses, and is about to reply, but I put my weight behind her and we hurry on. The tunnel though devoid of any source of illumination never goes into complete darkness. I can still easily see my way along the path, and know where the water's edge is by the light ridges of the ripples as they drift across the glassy surface. There will likely be a boat or barge along the waterway soon, disturbing the heavy stillness and quiet.

"I've been watching you." Says a heap of rubbish in a guttural accent that very clearly developed in eastern Europe. Once again I jump a little, clutching onto Nell, who doesn't seem to be surprised at all by the sudden appearance of a talking heap of rags and tatters. One big pale eye peers at us from amongst matted hair, and a big grin spreads across what this person uses as a face. The smell of her drifts slowly up my nose, and I gag slightly. She smells of stagnant pond water and mouldering food.

"Pasternak?" Lady Nell asks.

"Neil?" The creature asks.

Lady Nell waves a hand dismissively, "No dear, *Nell*. This is Rowan."

As the heap of detritus begins to move about, I can see that she is a very old woman. Her clothes are rags and tattered fabric, and every inch of her is stained with dirt and grime.

"I know you. You know me." Pasternak nods, "You were good friend with the poor dead boy."

"You knew Lawrence?" I ask.

"Who is Lawrence?" Pasternak tilts her head to one side quizzically, "I speak of Odd boy."

My heart stops beating for a moment. The world slows and I can't take a breath. Luckily for me Lady Nell takes the lead.

"What do you mean 'odd boy'?" She demands, looming over the much smaller woman.

Pasternak wags a finger at Nell, grinning. She holds out her other hand, palm up, open, expectant. She requires payment for information.

From her bulging pockets Nell pulls the gilded trinket she pilfered from Mandelbaum's Practice.

The crone takes it in her crooked fingers, turning it over and looking at it from every angle, "What is?" She asks suspiciously.

"Haven't a clue." Nell admits, "Some scientific contrivance."

"I have no need for it." Pasternak shoves the item back into Nell's hands, and snatches a piece of red silk from her pocket. Nell takes it back and slaps the old woman over the knuckles.

"It's rude to snatch."

"Please?" Pasternak bows her head in apology, rubbing the back of her slapped hand.

Begrudgingly, Nell hands over the red silk.

The old woman dabs the fine cloth on her cheek, her eyes closed and smiling, "Such pretty."

"Now," Nell says, loudly, "Explain yourself."

"Odd Boy. You call him that. He told me about De-Veire boy's tragedy. Now he is tragedy too."

The hairs on my neck stand on end, and suddenly the darkness of the tunnel is oppressive and stifling. I need to get out and breathe in the fresh air. I need light and open space.

"Oddly Brown has been murdered too?" Nell hisses,

"Where? When? Tell me!"

The crone shakes her head, and melts into the shadows. Nell, ranting and cursing goes after her, but can find no trace of the craggy old woman.

"Come back here!" Her thrashing about does nothing but mask any sounds made by Pasternak making her getaway.

My knees shake and almost give way under me.

"I need to get out." I mumble, turn and run.

I need to get out of the tunnel right now.

I need to get out of this dark, cramped, watery hole under the city. I pass both couples, still firmly engaged in each other, and stumble, slip and trip my way out into the dim misty light of Manchester.

I stop and lean on a wall, breathing deeply, my eyes shut tight. My racing heart begins to slow, and my insides judder as a surge of emotion crashes up me. I blurt out a noise; half sob half shout.

Opening my eyes I am unsurprised to find the Dear Departed sat on the steps, his hands on his knees, staring at me.

"What do you want?" I ask bitterly.

He smiles.

"Well?"

"I want to look after you." He says.

"What good can you do? You're a figment of my imagination."

He laughs at me.

91

It feels as though there is nothing else in the world now. Just us two at this water's edge. With my back against the wall at the side of the canal, it is a cold, hard, heavy reassuringly solid and very real presence.

"I've just been told that Oddly has been killed."

Lawrie's brow furrows, "I'm not sure who told you that, but it's not true."

"And you would know?"

"Yes. I would know."

Lady Nell emerges from the darkness of the tunnel, her heeled shoes making sudden loud clacking noises on the uneven floor.

"If I ever see that old woman again, I'll ring her neck for vanishing like that, sure as eggs!" Uncharacteristically for Lady Nell, she stops talking, her mouth hanging open.

She stares at me.

Past me.

She is looking at the Dear Departed!

She blinks dramatically twice, wafting her long eyelashes, then points at the apparition, "It's Lawrie!"

"Hold on a minute," I stumble over my words, "You can see him? But he's a figment of my imagination!"

"Rowan dear, your imagination isn't *that* good."

"Hello Nell." Lawrie says cheerfully, then vanishes.

Nell hurries up to where he was perched, feeling the steps and looking about as if he is simply hiding from her, and playing a silly prank, "That was Lawrie." She says again and again.

"That was Lawrie's ghost." I correct her. "Oh, and he told me that Oddly isn't actually dead."

Chapter Six

Madame Miasma

Nell stares at me agog as I recount the events of my recent peculiar days, and my frequent visitations from the spirit of the Dear Departed.

Shoving me hard in the shoulder, she cries out,

"Why didn't you tell me?"

"To be honest, I was beginning to think I was loosing my mind. I wasn't sure if you'd believe me. Edgar didn't."

"Oh that old cod? Don't mind a word that comes out of his mouth. He's not a believer in such things."

"You are? You were?"

"Always have been!" Nell laughs loudly, throwing back her head, "This is so ripe!" A thought occurs to her, and she grins from ear to mother-of-pearl studded ear, "I have an idea!"

I am practically dragged across the city by Lady Nell, her strong grip on my arm. I am marched to her Place. She hurries me up the steps and into the attic space that is her alcoholic domain.

A bar tender sits reading a book, as the single customer lays half asleep on a cushion by the stage. I am whisked into the rear of the establishment, into her bedroom-come-kitchen-come-store room, and deposited unceremoniously upon her bed.

I am dishevelled and crumpled from being manhandled across the city, and attempt to straighten myself out. Nell is rifling through her accumulated piles of miscellaneous trinkets and cheap treasures, frantically searching, but for what she will not say. Eventually she cries out triumphantly, holding up a small square of card. It is dog-eared, stained and vaguely pink. On one side is an elegantly scripted name and some basic information, decorated around with stars and moons in red ink. I read the card.

Madame Miasma. Clairvoyant. Spiritualist. Medium.

"Really? I'm not sure how this will help."

"Can't hurt to give it a bash, though, eh?"

"I suppose."

"That's the spirit!" She chuckles, "Forgive the pun."

I stare at the pink card in my hand, trying to decipher the small writing. It's an address.

"This is ridiculous." I hand the card to Nell.

"Seeing a spectre is ridiculous. Getting a Medium involved seems common sense to me."

"No, not that. This woman's address."

"What of it?"

"It's *my* address." Nell and I both stare at the card.

"Sure as eggs, so it is!"

The bar tender pokes his head into our incredulous moment, "Sorry to bother you, Nell. Had a message come through about a Ball. They want us to provide the wet. All good?"

Nell dismisses the man with a wave of her hand,

"Yes yes, get all the details for me?"

He nods, and removes himself to his position behind the bar.

"Now," She breathes, "Shall we visit Madame Miasma? It *is* on your way home."

As we make our way once more across the city, I struggle to keep pace with Nell. My feet ache and I am tired. My body and mind are finding all of this strangeness a little bit too much. One moment I am up and full of energy, the next I feel the crushing weight of the world. Without some kind of a balance, I worry that I may become delirious.

Glad that we are at least heading homeward, my feet and I breathe a little easier. I will soak them in warm soapy water and rub them with talc as a treat this evening.

"Who else lives in your building?" Nell queries.

I think over my years spent living in my little attic room, and draw mostly a blank, "Everyone keeps to themselves." I rub my hands together to push out the misty chill from my bones, "There's the landlady Mrs Taffeta, and a young woman called Tiffin. Aside from them I don't recall ever meeting any of the other tenants."

"How very mysterious. Could it be your landlady?"

"She is a very odd person. It could be." I very much hope that Madame Miasma is not the secret mystical identity of Mrs Taffeta. I try my very best to avoid her, for good reason. I do not want to involve her in anything personal, least of all something so unusual as my current situation.

I let us into the building, and the familiar smell of damp, body odour and cigarette smoke greats me. All of these things emanate from Mrs Taffeta, who is busy sweeping the dirt from one side of the entrance hall to the other, and back again. She does this whenever she thinks there is a conversation worth eavesdropping into. An argument can be heard from one of the first floor rooms. A man and a woman.

"They've been at it all morning." Mrs Taffeta sucks on her cigarette, letting the ash fall to the floor, "She's been having it away with some sailor visiting from Liverpool."

Eyeing up the two of us, Mrs Taffeta pauses sweeping and leans on the weather-warped broom. She is wary of me, clearly unsure how I will behave toward her due to our most recent encounter, "You know you can't have a lady up in your room. You're not married. It'd be indecent. Not having that in my house."

Nell sighs, "He wouldn't know where to start with a lady, so we're all quite safe in that regard. Who is Madame Miasma?"

The old lady blinks slowly, trying to process the information. She gives up and retreats to her natural position of idle gossip and boring conversation, "They had a whole set of new bed sheets delivered last week. Can't imagine they'll have seen much use, what with her getting a jolly rogering."

"Mrs Taffeta, someone who lives here with us works as a Medium, and her name is Madame Miasma."

Thin shoulders shrug at me, "Don't know any Miasma."

"I do." Tiffin stands lightly on a step near the first floor landing, leaning on the rickety bannister. She holds her nose in the air, and shakes her shoulders a little, making the tassels on her shawl swish too and fro, "I am Madame Miasma. You'd better come up." She turns and indicates the door to her room.

I caution my friend on the state of the stairs, and my warning is punctuated by an indignant grunt from the Landlady. Taking the lead, and showing Nell where she can safely step without threat of injury, we scale the treacherous path up to the first floor.

Madame Miasma's room is much more plush than my own. The ceiling is high, and painted pastel green. The wallpaper is patterned foliage, and everything else is a varying shade of pink. The room is divided into a bedroom and a living space by a rose Chinese patterned folding screen. On everything there are fuchsia scarfs and coral shawls and blush sheets draped limply.

Candles are fixed to many surfaces without candleholders, the molten cadaver of previous beeswax tapers the base of the next. The room is heavy with a scent like treacle. It is sickly sweet, and makes the atmosphere uncomfortable and sticky.

The young woman has thickly applied mascara, framing her eyes with lashes clumped into barbs. She flops herself clumsily onto the shell-pink chaise lounge with an attempt at graceful mystique, removing an hourglass from its place, lain on a tasseled cushion to make herself more comfortable. She flicks open a worn cigarette case, lifting one of the sticks to her lips, and leans into a nearby candle to light it.

"Care for one?" She says through tight-lipped puffs.

"No, thank you." I say, looking for somewhere to sit.

There is no free surface. The table and chairs in her sectioned living space are covered not only with fabric, but books and colourful rocks and assorted bound clumps of twigs and leaves.

I stumble over a pile of scarves and large playing cards, scattering them sideways under the table, "Oh! Sorry."

"It's fine. Leave it."

Nell flicks closed a book laying open nearby, and her eyebrows raise dramatically at the title. Tiffin coughs daintily, her eyes very clearly saying to the both of us *'stop touching my stuff'*.

"I admire your sense of homely decor. You might have gone overboard with the draperies though." Nell moves away from the alarming book, producing the square of card that bears the Medium's name and address.

Tiffin takes it from her and looks it over, "Not had anyone actually take notice of one of my cards before. Usually it's just word of mouth that provides me with business. I am *The Great Madame Miasma*."

She would sound much grander if her accent didn't scream common-as-muck Mancunian, I think. It is a warm and friendly voice, nonetheless.

The chaise longue has seen better days, it creaks a

little as she shifts her weight, and the arm is almost thread-bare.

"I thought you were called Tiffin?" I say.

Tutting, she shakes her head, "No. Well, yes I am. Angelica Tiffin. But professionally, which is the capacity you are visiting me in; I am *The Great Madame Miasma*."

"Why do you make such strange noises in the communal bathroom?" I ask the question out loud instead of in my own head, and at once wish the ground to open up and swallow me. An embarrassed flush of blood rushes to my cheeks, and I mumble an apology while fidgeting my hands at my face.

Nell laughs. Loudly.

Tiffin stares at me, her face somewhere between shock and amusement. After an eternal moment of tension, she smiles, and my embarrassment fades a fraction.

"It's all to do with mirrors." She says by way of explanation, which is no explanation at all, "Now, what do you want? And by the way, I count this as a consultation, and I charge by the hour." She picks up the hourglass, and turns it over.

"Wait, I haven't-"

Nell shushes me, "Rowan, tell the nice Spiritualist about your haunting."

Tiffin begins to lean forward, "Oh yes, do."

"It started the day of his funeral. He appeared to me initially at the window of our room upstairs. He's appeared four times now over the last day or so."

"Upstairs?" Tiffin looks up, as if she is trying to see through several floors into my room high above, "Does he float about? Does he moan and drag his feet? Does he cry and sob? Does he wail terribly?"

The young woman is eager for some dreadful gory detail, and I feel my lacklustre retelling of his visitations will put her off from engaging with us, "No. He just talks. He tries to offer me advice. I think he's trying to look after me."

Miasma leans back upon her chaise thoughtfully.

"He has appeared to you in multiple locations?"

"Yes. At Edgar's and by the canal as well."

"So it's not a place that is being haunted, but a person. How very different."

Nell makes a show of resting her head down onto my shoulder and pouting, "Poor lover boys can't be separated, even by the cold kiss of the grave."

I brush her off.

"A seance." Tiffin muses, "Yes I think that should do the trick. We can conjure the dead boy and banish him."

"No, I don't want to banish him."

"You like being haunted? Each to their own. So what do you want me for?"

"He was killed. I want to know who did it."

Tiffin sucks deeply and protractedly on her cigarette, staring me out, "I see." She says finally, "Then we will need four people known to the deceased, plus yourself. And lots of space. A big room. And mirrors. It must be private. Can you provide this?"

I look at Nell for guidance. My room upstairs will be no good for such an event, and I doubt Nell's Place would ever see its door locked, so private; it is not.

"Edgar will host us." She says, nodding.

"He will?"

"I'll see to it. Madame Miasma, you shall receive payment at the close of the event. Until then you may have this as a gesture of our good intentions." Nell hands over the trinket pilfered from Mandelbaum's consultation room.

Tiffin takes it and turns it over in her hands, examining it, "What is it?"

"Haven't a clue. Some valuable scientific contrivance. Worth a great deal of money."

"How much?"

"Lots."

Nell nods a curt bow and begins to sweep me from the room, "I will forward the address, time and date to you via Rowan once arranged!" She closes the door firmly after us and teeters hurriedly down the stairs.

Mrs Taffeta makes a great show of sweeping the landing, pretending that she was not listening at the door.

"Where are you going?" I ask Nell's back.

"To make arrangements. I have a seance and a Ball to arrange! What an exciting day today has been! I'm fired up like a bowlful of horseradish!" As she clips away on her little heeled shoes, she talks animatedly to herself, gesticulating excitedly and laughing.

Before closing the front door she turns to me grinning, "We're going to have such fun!"

Slam.

"You don't look like you're much up for fun." Mrs Taffeta mutters, casting a sideways look my way as she pushes past to descend the stairs. Now that the entertainment is over I am of little interest to her.

Fun is not a word I would use to describe how I feel about a seance. I approach it with trepidation. Yes, that's the right word. Trepidation. Unease. Disquiet. Those are good too. My aching feet remind me of my promises to them, and so I make my way up to my room.

Days pass without event. I spend one evening helping out at Nell's Place behind the bar, earning myself a few coins for food and rent for the next week. The Balls bring in plenty of money for Nell when she provides for them, and so she generously hands me a little extra to cover Lawrie's share of the bills too. She advises me to begin searching for a new lodger to share my room, and though I nod and agree, I find myself reluctant to have someone else take up the bed of the recently deceased. I am more inclined to move out and find somewhere new rather than remain in that room, with only the memories of our happy days.

The secondary reason for my thoughts turning to new lodgings is the deceitful Mrs Taffeta. Harmless enough, I had thought. Yet she had allowed a stranger into my room. A thief! A violation of my private, intimate space.

The evening spent tending the bar is, all in all, a welcome distraction from the unusual events of the previous

days. I serve warm beer, cloudy cider, large measures of
Nell's bathtub brewed gin, and make small talk with many of
the customers.

Some are faces I have seen and served before. Many
are not. A sea of faces; men, women, undecided, young, old,
all of them as estranged from the mundane world around
them as myself.

Some men wear paint on their faces, fluttering fans
and chirping merrily like sparrows in a fruiting hedgerow.
One corner holds a group of women in slacks and plain
shirts, looking all the world like teenage boys, putting on a
good show of machismo and boyish swagger. The stage is
occupied by a singer and a small band. She sings saucy
songs, flashing a thigh now and again to garner a little more
attention from a crowd very much wrapped up in its own
conversations and intrigue.

"Wine please, my good boy!"

I turn to the customer addressing me. Through the
pale paint and red powder on the cheeks I see the little face
of Doctor Mandelbaum peering out at me. It takes him several moments to recognise me. Once he does, it is obvious.
His face drops, and a cold dead terror fixes in his eyes,

"*You!*"

I pretend that I have not noticed who he is, and pour
him a glass of wine. It is more like vinegar, but I have been
told that after the second glass, everything served at Nell's
Place tastes like that, and you get used to it.

"There you are." I hand him the wine, and take payment. The little man seems relieved that I have not spoken of our encounter, or the information he gave away.

Seizing this opportunity to speak once more with a Whisperer, even if it is the fretful Mandelbaum, I close my hand on his as he takes his change. I lean forward and speak, just quiet enough for him to hear, "Oddly Brown. I need to know he's safe. Pass it on."

Mandelbaum pulls his hand from mine and hurries away, leaving his wine behind. I watch him retreat through the lapping tide of people, and hurry out of the door into the cold night.

Beside me, impatient punters rap knuckles on the bar top, "Hey, you serving?"

"Watcha, fungus. Vada where you're waving your fambles. You've capsized my bevvie!"

I return to serving drinks and clearing up spillages, mentally crossing my fingers that Mandelbaum can live up to his reputation as a blabbermouth.

After my hours working are complete, I take opportunity to rest in Nell's semi-private room behind the bar. She is going over orders and invoices and letters and notes, scribbling on some of them then stacking them away. Others cause her to tick something off her list, then to toss the letter or invoice into her small fire.

"Keeping out of mischief?" I ask her, as I lay myself out slowly onto the pile of mattresses and cushions she uses as a bed.

"Not for long, sugarplum!" Her usual verbosity is

absent, as she is focussed entirely on her preparations for the Ball.

From previous experience I know that these arrangements will have to be made anonymously with a great many people and organisations. The host venue, the band, the waiting staff, the dissemination of information regarding time and location to the right people, in the right places, in the correct coded ways. It is a tricky operation, made especially fraught due to the constant fear of the Constabulary discovering the Ball and arresting all those in attendance.

I talk to Nell of the seance, though it is more to myself than to her, "We need four people known to Lawrie, plus myself. So you, Edgar and Saffron. We need one more. Who else did he know that won't think all of this to be utter madness?"

"He knew a great many people."

"Yes, but who would attend the seance with us?"

"You will work the Ball for me, won't you Rowan, dear? I need a face I can rely on by my side"

"Anything you need."

"Just waiting on tables for the most part. But a bit of everything."

I nod.

I need the money, and the Balls are always a lot of fun. The frisson of danger and the secrecy around them make them all the more exciting and special, "But who else should we invite to the seance?"

Nell has returned to her pile of notes and invoices,

ignoring me now that she has secured my commitment to working the event.

"Who could we invite that won't think us all totally mad? Hmm?"

Nell tuts at me, "Mad?"

"For holding a seance!"

"Go home, Rowan! Go home and get your head down and sleep. I'm busy."

I rise, give her a gentle hug, and depart.

When I arrive back in my room, I curl up in my bed and make the most of the few hours of darkness that remain to get some sleep. My dreams are filled with strange visions of Nell in chains, Edgar stripped of his fine clothes, begging for scraps in a gutter, blood curdling over fresh wounds, and the Dear Departed conjured as a fiendish ghoul.

I am awoken from these disturbing dreams by a knock knock knock. Wrapping myself hurriedly in my dressing gown, I open the door and am greeted by a cloud of cigarette smoke exhaled from the lips of Mrs Taffeta.

"These came for you."

I waft away the foul smelling words as she hands me a parcel wrapped in brown paper and string, and a letter in a white envelope. The handwriting on the letter is Edgar's. The handwriting on the parcel is unknown to me.

"Thank you." Mrs Taffeta lingers at the door as I slowly close it. Her nosy nature getting the best of her, she is clearly hoping for me to open the package in front of her. I have no such intention, "Good morning."

I close the door, and listen. After a little huff I hear her slippered feet shuffle away and down the stairs. Returning to my bed I take a seat cross legged on my dishevelled duvet, and begin to unwrap the parcel. Inside is a small note.

A fine suit, for a fine young man. I hope it serves you well. Porte-le avec fierté. Tremblay.

I lift the folded items from their paper trappings. The suit is indeed very fine. A deep brown jacket and waistcoat in a soft tweed with blue satin lining, alongside some crisply pressed matching trousers. I've never owned an item of clothing so well made, let alone made specifically for me. It is surely the most expensive thing I now own. Again I wonder what I might owe the Frenchman.

Edgar's letter is opened next, and it is equally as brief. A date and time for the evening of light refreshments and sophisticated chinwagging with the DeVeire family that we are invited to. Auspicious that this wonderful gift arrived today, I will thankfully not need to borrow one of Edgar's old mothballed suits.

A little thrill of nervous excitement passes over me. I jump up, dig out my nicest white shirt, and put it on with my new suit. It fits very well. I look at myself this way and that in my grimy mirror.

It is quite flattering, and I smile.

Chapter Seven

Merry Belles and Prison Cells

A week passes by with little excitement. I seem to be abandoned by the Dear Departed. I speak to him often, but I know not if he can hear me, or even if he is lingering still. His absence brings the pain of his loss back into stark relief.

Nell is busy with the Ball preparations, and Edgar is out of the city for a business meeting of some kind. So I waste time on sleepless nights wandering the streets, willing some dramatic situation upon myself, hoping that Lawrie will appear to me again.

The rain-smeared visage of the city drips in grey and brown daubs, smudged and undefined. Lights in windows and shop fronts are stars in the vast night of the city. I fall into a melancholy mood, and allow myself to paddle a little in a brook of my own morbid and lonely thoughts.

In an attempt to shake myself out of my maudlin grump, I take myself shopping. Today's varieties of rain switch from Light Misting to Sudden Downpour at unpredictable intervals.

With the small amount of money I have left from Nell's generosity, I purchase a cheap umbrella and then a cup of tea at a small cafe with big windows. I sit and watch the people rushing hither and thither in the changeable weather, and am thankful for the warm brew in my belly.

During a lightening of today's deluge, I shift from the cafe and visit several boutiques selling various ranges of men's attire. I need a neck tie and nice shoes to go with my new suit. The tie is easy to acquire. The shoes require visits to several addresses, before I decide that the first pair I tried on are actually the best ones by far, and return to purchase them. With the ensemble complete, I feel better about the approaching meeting with the DeVeire family, though the worry bubbling in my gut regarding how the Dear Departed's brother will take to my presence is a lurking menace.

One thing at a time, I tell myself.

First, the Ball!

The night of the much anticipated Ball arrives, and after meeting Nell at her Place, we take a taxi cab to the venue. Tucked away amongst broad red-brick mills and factories just north of the city centre we find the building that shall host the revelry. It is squat, and seems to be compressed into odd shapes by the bulk of the structures around it. The air tastes of coal smoke and the sweat of a hard day's work.

"I've had people in all day getting the place scrubbed up." Nell grins. She is dressed in her finest beaded flapper gown, in a vivid shade of amber. She wears a band around her head with golden feathers in, and an expensive pair of silk stockings, "Don't I look delicious! I'm sure to be the belle of the Ball!" Nell is giddy with excitement and nervous energy, eager for the frivolity to begin.

I am not so finely attired. My new suit is awaiting the DeVeire soiree, and so I am wearing my good black suit. The one I wore for Lawrie's funeral, once again with a sprig of Lavender in my lapel.

In very short shrift the guests will begin arriving, and so we hurry into the building to make the final preparations. In the entrance the walls have been decorated with garlands of fabric flowers and candles. The large room beyond is divided into two unequally sized parts by an enormous red curtain. In the smaller portion of the room is the bar and a small stage area. Here is where the drinks will be prepared, and where the band will play. The larger portion is dotted at its periphery with round tables and almost-matching chairs. There is a large open space in the centre for dancing and, I suspect, cavorting to boot. This side of the room is also decorated with fabric garlands and candles.

"It looks lovely."

"I know." Nell grins, taking in the ambience of the room, "The musicians will be arriving at the back door. Let them in would you?" Nell begins to occupy herself by fussing at flowers that aren't sat exactly as she likes.

Moving into the smaller, undecorated part of the room, I find a rear door and beyond that the large double doors that lead out onto a yard. Indeed the musicians are waiting, sat upon their instrument cases.

"In you come, chaps." I call to them happily.

My cheery tones fall on deaf ears. They have evidently been waiting for some time. Shifting quickly into the dry and warm interior, I show them to where they are to set up, and receive some very quizzical looks.

"What's with the curtain?" The drummer asks.

Nell sweeps up to them, all smiles and wide arm movements, "I am pleased as punch to have you here! You came highly recommended. Lots of upbeat, toe-tapping stuff, if you please. Tonight will be just cinnamon!"

"Something odd going on?" The drummer moves toward the curtain but Nell takes him by the arm, steering him back to his set-up.

"Sometimes it is prudent to be heard and not seen." She stage-whispers.

"You don't want us to see who's here?" Asks a small man with a big brass instrument.

Nell nods, "It's safer that way. For you and for them. Enough questions, time is running short. Hurry and get strumming and blowing and so on. Music! Music at once"

Before long the band strikes up and begins to play as the first attendees arrive. Gowns, tiaras, extravagant suits, cloaks, walking canes, fans, perfume and wigs adorn all manner of people, exaggerating and semi-disguising their more mundane everyday appearances. In delicate considered rebellion to the social constructs which restrict them from freely expressing themselves, the men, women and those unbound from gender wear whatever they please and however it pleases them at the Balls. They wear trousers, or dresses, apply makeup or draw on a moustache. They flirt, they laugh and with their edifice decorated how it pleases them, they wear themselves more comfortably than anywhere or anytime else. Many of the attendees wear lavender about their person, or a green carnation, and some women carry posies of violets.

I busy myself with taking drinks orders, relaying them to the others who are making them, then balancing them precariously on silver plated trays to take to the painted and decorated party goers. Back and forth, back and forth I go, occasionally taking time to chat with or be flirted with by someone who has already had a few beverages before arriving.

Edgar and Saffron arrive, and I hug them both tightly. They are dressed immaculately, and wear horned and hook-nosed disguises as if at a masquerade.

"It's good to see you!" Edgar pats me heartily on the back, "Nell tells me I am to host a little occult gathering for you." His tone is serious but there is a teasing smirk on his face.

"It's all her idea."

"I didn't doubt it."

After the initial hours where greetings and introductions are made, once thoroughly lubricated, the first of the attendees take to dancing. A handful of them know the modern dance craze that is the Charleston, and before long even those in hooped skirts in the style of a layered cake are up and swinging.

Nell is in her element; Flitting like a moth from the light of one conversation to the next, leaving when it loses her interest, or when she overhears something else which piques it.

"You're a dishy feely ome."

"Thank you."

The man addressing me is made excessively tall by a gargantuan white powdered wig. His face is painted as pale as his hairpiece, and his lips and cheeks have been smeared with vivid red lipstick. I smile politely and move to a group whose glasses look particularly empty.

"Anything else to drink?" I ask.

From the rear of the building, from some unseen place comes a soft crash, and the musicians falter then stop.

Across the sea of people I feel Nell's eyes on me. We both hurry across the room, between the dancers, and behind the curtain.

"Keep playing." Nell's tone is a needle, and she jabs a finger at the band, who hesitate a moment before their lead counts them back in.

The crash was the sound of stacked crates being upset by the stumbling entrance of a very wet trio of uninvited guests.

One is curled up on the floor. He seems to have fallen or been dropped upon the crates, and is responsible for the noisy disturbance. The other two are attempting to help the prostrate individual to his feet.

"We need to find Lady Nell." One of them says to the room in general. She is a small, delicate looking girl. Her voice is quiet and apologetic.

"You've found her." Nell strides over, taking hold of the two bedraggled people. They stink, and she tells them as much.

They nod, and apologise, cowering before the gilded storm cloud, "It's from the canal." Says the girl of the smell, "Had to dive in to fish him out."

While Nell is focussed on the duo before her, I move to the prone form on the floor. He is curled into a foetal position, soaked to the bone and dirty all over. There appears to be bruising on his exposed arms, and if it weren't for his shallow breathing I might have thought him a corpse.

"It's Oddly!" I shout, rushing to wipe the dirt from his face. I run my hands all over him, feeling for any other injuries or wounds.

He is in a bad way, frozen and pale.

Nell pins the two before her with her painted talons.

"Tell me everything!"

"We heard that Oddly was missing, that people were looking for him." The girl stutters.

"We went looking. Found him half dead not an hour ago. Been unconscious in the canal, wedged up between a boat and the walkway for god knows how long." Her fellow explains as fast as he can, tripping over his words to get them out, "Surprised he's still ticking."

Oddly slowly opens his eyes, looking at me with surprise, before passing out.

"We need to get him somewhere warm. We need a Doctor." I say, worried that he might die before we can do anything for him.

"Had to come in the back way." The boy stutters,

"The front-"

"Every man for himself." Edgar and Saffron hurry past the curtain and freeze when they see us.

"What?" Nell scowls at them, her eyes ablaze.

Whistles and shouting.

The slamming of doors and the heavy thundering of big boots. Cries and screams and shouts of indignation reach us swiftly from the other side of the curtain.

"Hilda Handcuffs." Nell grimaces at me, "Get this lot out, quickly as possible. There's a way into the building next door from the cellar. Hide there 'til it's clear. Go to my Place."

The band and bar staff have already fled. As soon as the sound of the Police forcing their way into the building reached our ears, they made their decision. Picking up what they could, they ran out of the back door.

"What are you going to do?" I ask Nell.

"What I do best," She smiles, "Cause a scandal."

"You'll be arrested!" I protest, thinking that to be the least of her worries if the police get hold of her.

"I've just got rid of one black eye, I had grown quite fond of it. I think it's time to try for another."

"Nell, don't be daft!" Edgar pleads with her, but she skirts him.

I kneel down and pull one of Oddly's arms up over my shoulders. The two who found him stand staring at me, unsure what to do.

"Help me, for pity's sake!" I grunt as I stand, lifting

Oddly's full weight. The two of them break from their stunned immobility, and help by sharing the load.

Saffron removes her mask, discarding it on the floor.

She lifts up the front of her long dress and takes the lead, "This way."

"Oi coppers!" Nell shouts loudly in a way I have never heard before, making her way back to the dance floor, "The entertainment has arrived!"

A police officer snarls at Nell, raising his truncheon to strike her. Before he can land the blow she jabs quickly at him with a fist, connecting it with his jaw and sending him sideways.

Glimpsed beyond Nell is a scene of fear. Attendees are on the floor, kicked, or struggling against being stripped by jeering and goading Constables; hounds and their red-furred quarry.

We hurry to the rear of the building, find the stairs to the cellar and make our way awkwardly down. The steps are stone, and the air grows colder as we descend.

I slip, nearly taking all six of us face first down the last few feet. The cellar is full of crates marked as containing tea, coffee, tinned food and more.

The sound of stamping and crying and shouting can still be made out through the thick wooden floorboards overhead.

"Which side do we choose? Which building next door are we supposed to get to?" Asks the boy.

I do not know, and so we split up. I search to our left,

while Edgar, also now removing his mask, takes the right. Saffron stays with Oddly and the wet couple. I search the walls until I find a doorway of a kind; a low arch and a passage beyond. Formally some sort of drainage tunnel I suspect.

"I think I've found it." I shout.

The others join me, Oddly now supported by Edgar and the wet boy. We crouch and slowly shuffle through the tunnel, dragging our unconscious friend as carefully as we can between us.

The tunnel stretches on for much longer than it should, and a frustrated claustrophobia begins to take hold of my chest.

I pull harder on Oddly, grunting for the others to hurry. Voices echo behind us. The police are searching the building. If they find us stuck in this tunnel we're sitting ducks. Our feet scuffing the floor, our clothes scraping and rustling against the tunnel walls, and my heartbeat in my ears is deafening. I am sure the Constables will locate us at any moment, drag us from our hiding place and beat us, and arrest us. Hounds after foxes.

Popping like a cork from a bottle, we emerge as a flailing heap of limbs into the cellar of the building next door.

Our tangle lays still for a moment, listening, until I wheeze for everyone to get off of me, and I can breathe again.

We wait a while, until we are sure that we are not being followed, and until we hear the voices and sound of police cars begin to fade away.

    With Oddly supported between Edgar and Myself, Saffron finds the way up and out, and trailing the two wet youths behind us, make our escape into the cold night.

    "You two, what are your names?" I ask.

    "I'm Buddy. This is my sister Violet." The boy says. The chill of the night and his very wet clothes are making him shiver.

    Edgar thanks them both for bringing Oddly to us with a handful of coins, "Now, fetch a Doctor. Bring him to Nell's Place. You know where that is?" He commands.

    "You know Doctor Mandelbaum?" I ask, to which Violet nods and Buddy shakes his head, "He won't like it, but fetch him." I take the lavender from my lapel and hand it over, "Give him this, tell him it is urgent."

    Saffron has managed to flag down a passing taxicab, and calls to us. We bundle Oddly in, much to the protests of the driver. A loud rebuff from Edgar and the promise of a generous tip persuade the him to overlook the very wet and very smelly creature slung between us.

    Violet and Buddy scamper away down a side street, and with a *rattlebang* the cab starts off. I sit back, and allow Oddly to slump onto my shoulder. His breathing is shallow and infrequent. We travel in a stunned silence for a time, each of us lost in our own thoughts.

    "Nell's an idiot." Edgar huffs.

    "I think she was very brave, to go back and face the coppers like that."

Saffron coughs lightly, and holds up a finger, shushing us both, "Now is not the time for arguments."

I stare down at Oddly, glad that he is not dead. Lawrie knew he was still alive. How did he know?

As we rock back and forth over an uneven portion of road, the boy becomes dislodged and slides further down me, resting his head on my chest. Under his cheek I can feel something in my inside pocket.

His note!

"I forgot all about it!" I exclaim.

"About what?" Edgar stares at me, baffled by my outburst.

I shift Oddly into a better position, and from my inside pocket pull out the note I was secretly given by the young man on the day of Lawrie's funeral.

I hand it to Edgar, "Oddly gave me this note ages ago. I forgot all about it, I couldn't decipher his handwriting."

Edgar fixes his monocle into place beneath his more expressive eyebrow, and examines the note, "His penmanship is appalling."

Saffron takes the note and squints at it, "It says; None of us are safe. I'm leaving the city for a while, and suggest you do the same. Beware the Nettle's sting. Stay Safe. Oddly."

"What happened to you?" I whisper in Oddly's ear. He doesn't respond, of course.

The cab arrives at Nell's Place, Edgar pays much more than he should do for the ride, and we sling Oddly's arms over our shoulders once more.

Saffron leads us up the stairs, and ushers a path through the small number of customers drinking there for us to take Oddly into Nell's private space behind the bar.

We lay him down on her bed, and as Saffron stokes the fire, I begin to strip Oddly of his wet clothes. His skin is discoloured all over by his time spent half-dead in the canal, and he is covered in bruises. I suspect he will have a broken bone or two as well, by the vivid purple discolouration on his ribs and legs.

We wrap him in as many blankets as we can find, and attempt to get him to drink some water. He wakes just enough to take a couple of small gulps, before coughing and once more retreating into unconsciousness. I sit staring at him, comatose and barely alive, trying not to imagine the pain and suffering he endured to be in this state.

"I will make some tea." Saffron busies herself putting together a pot on the stove, and Edgar exhales heavily through his nose, clearly deep in his own pondering.

I sit on the bed beside the swaddled Oddly, put my arm around him and pull him in close to me. I hope my added body heat will help to restore him in some way.

By the warmth of the fire, and from the lulling of the adrenaline from my blood I begin to nod off.

I am shaken gently awake by Edgar, and through bleary tired eyes I see the small shape of a very disgruntled

Doctor Mandelbaum at the rear of the room. He carries with him a leather case, and has a stethoscope slung behind his neck.

"He's alive?" Mandelbaum glares at Oddly from across the room, "After how long in the canal?"

"You came. Thank you." I murmur, as I rise, being careful not to disturb Oddly too much.

"Yes. I did." He tosses the lavender at me angrily, "Keep your weeds." Kneeling in front of Oddly, he undoes the tight blankets and begins to examine his body, listening to his breathing and his heart, laying his hands over his limbs and joints, feeling for breaks and fractures and wounds.

From his leather case he produces a bottle of tablets, and another of thick green liquid. He feeds the green liquid into Oddly's mouth via a spoon, and hands me the tablets.

"His recovery will be long. He will likely sleep much of the next week until his body is restored enough to handle consciousness. He will need to take one of these pills every day, they will help to fight off any infections or poisons in his system from his time in the water."

"Thank you."

Mandelbaum pulls a small book from his pocket and makes a note in it, then writes in another book, from which he tears the page and hands it to me.

It is his bill, which I cannot afford.

Mandelbaum packs away his paraphernalia into its case, and stands watching me.

"Can I owe you?" I ask.

"No."

Edgar takes the bill from me, cocking an eyebrow at the diminutive Doctor, "Seems excessive, old chap." He says in a low voice.

Mandelbaum's eye twitches, and his fists clench. He would dearly love to give us all a piece of his mind, I have no doubt, but being in the presence of someone with a social standing as high as Edgar's, he is making the wise decision to hold his tongue.

Shrugging, Edgar writes the Doctor a cheque, which is snatched from his hand as he rushes out of the bar.

"Today is proving to be a very expensive day." Edgar murmurs to himself, putting away his cheque book.

The dim light of dawn is making its way into the room, and there are no sounds of customers at Nell's Place. There is only Edgar, Oddly and myself here.

"Where's Saffron?"

"Spending more money. At the police station."

"What's she buying there?"

"Freedom."

I am confused, and my sleepy head can't quite catch up with the conversation, "Sorry?"

Edgar eases himself into a chair, sighing wearily,

"I have a contact or two at the Police Station. Sometimes a few quid slipped to the right people can work miracles."

My brain begins to catch up, "You've bribed them to let people free that were arrested at the Ball?"

"No. Only Nell. I'm not *that* rich. They can overlook one, when they have so many."

"You have Police contacts?" I scratch my head, "So you knew they wouldn't listen to me about the journal, because..."

"Because I had already made a telephone call regarding that fact."

"You still let me go down there?"

"I tried to persuade you not to, but you wouldn't listen! Now, Nell will likely not be released until mid morning, and I can't be seen to be meeting her."

"I'll need to?"

Edgar nods.

"Ok."

"Take her a change of clothes, she'll need something fresher that what they'll have put her in."

After attempting to sleep, and failing, I begin to pack some clothes into a satchel for Nell.

A blouse and skirt and coat and a hat.

I hope they will be a good choice for her, as even in the face of arrest and under the scrutiny of uncaring Police eyes, I am sure that she will want to look her very best.

Edgar stays with Oddly as I make my way across the city to the Station.

There are fewer Constables around today, and I feel less like I am a piece of meat under hungry eyes. The Desk Sergeant is surprised to see me.

"I'm here for Nell." I say.

He looks over his ledgers and nods, "Ah yes." He waves over a young Constable, "Release Neil Protea."

Lady Nell appears a minute later, in a most unusual state. She is dressed in the rough grey trousers and blue wool shirt issued to male prisoners. Her fine clothes are gone, has some rather alarming five o'clock shadow, has a split lip, bruised arm, and is limping.

"I bought you a change of clothes."

Nell rests an arm across my shoulders, using me for support, "Thank you, pudding." She says, "How's Oddly?"

"He'll live."

"Fantabulosa."

Chapter Eight

His Beloved Mother

It is common knowledge among those closest to Lady Nell that she has had more than one life. Like a cat, incidents that would have felled any normal man or woman proved to be near misses with Death's scythe. Her first life was the one in which she grew up, rebelled and left home. This had been in the body and under the name given to her by her parents, and they hadn't suited her very well.

After the scythe came close once or twice, she decided to find a name and a life that fit her better, and so Lady Nell came into being. Or rather, came to the fore. She had always been there, but hidden away.

Public toilets in the entrance of the Police Station become a changing room, and the male attire given to her is changed for the clothes I brought with me.

"They're not what I'd have picked, but it'll do for the walk home." She says as we slip away.

She is covering the lower half of her face with the collar of her coat, and her large sunglasses hide her baggy tired eyes.

Despite being in obvious pain, Nell seems in high spirits. It is a front. It is a thin veneer, well cracked. Sudden noises and people approaching around corners give her small frights. Her nerves are frayed, and she leans heavily on me.

"Guess what arrived the other day?" I had forgotten

to tell her, what with the excitement of the Ball, "My new suit!"

"You didn't let me guess." She chides me, amusedly, "Tell me, is it wonderful? Do you look simply delicious in it?"

"Like you'd come back for seconds."

This makes her laugh, and she winces, clutching at her side. I suspect a broken rib.

It isn't a long walk back to Nell's Place across the city centre, but today it feels like a million miles. We take our time, and soon enough I have Nell laid on her bed next to Oddly, where she promptly falls fast asleep, snoring loudly.

I daren't summon Mandelbaum again, and so I decide to leave Nell to rest and recuperate, one of her bar tenders playing Nurse.

Oddly's condition looks to be no different than last night, but the smell of the canal has been rinsed away, and he looks human again.

I linger a moment, and wonder where he was going, when he passed me that note. I wonder who stopped him. How was I to beware the Nettle's sting? Here he is, near death, black and blue and hardly breathing. Victim to the Nettle's sting?

I am not a religious man, but I speak a little prayer to whichever deity might be listening. Just in case. I pray for his recovery.

I spend the next few days surreptitiously stealing away the morning editions before Mrs Taffeta has chance to notice. I run my finger over the advertisements that ask for lodgers. There are many available, but none so conveniently situated as where I currently reside. There are many in Northenden, a trove in Ashton, a plethora in Withington, and a deluge of available rooms in Levenshulme. None of them quite fit the bill. Perhaps I should employ someone to fit a new lock to my door, refuse to give Mrs Taffeta a key, and stay put. Perhaps.

I stack the papers in a corner of the room, and carefully dress in my lovely new suit. I marvel at how well it fits. I don't often think of myself as attractive. It seems self-indulgent. But in these figure hugging garments, perfectly tailored to the curves of my body, I do. I feel attractive. I feel worth something. It is a new and unexpected feeling, and find myself pondering what the Dear Departed would make of me, if he materialised now and came upon me looking a swell. I hope he'd like what he saw. His opinion always meant a great deal. He paid attention. He noticed things. His compliments, when offered, always made my heart flutter, and I would blush.

I brush my hair, slicking it with wax, and decide that I am ready. What exactly I'm ready for I won't know until I arrive at the DeVeire front door. Firstly though, I must meet Edgar.

He tries to give me helpful hints and tips in the taxi-cab ride. *Don't* say such-and-such, *do* speak with this-or-other, *don't* hold cutlery like an ape. He goes on and on, preparing me. I wonder if perhaps he thinks I might be very uncouth and make a show of him. I'm not that much of an uncultured scruffian.

"Don't worry." I reassure him in one brief pause for breath, "I won't speak unless spoken to, I plan to stay out of the way, I won't get drunk. All I really want to do is give his Beloved Mother back his things, then we can leave."

Edgar nods, "Good man."

The DeVeire pile isn't very far from Edgar and Saffron's home. The taxicab moves into leafier lanes, where the houses become detached, and set further back from the road.

Then high walls rise up, manicured hedges and iron fencing segregate the large estates. We turn off the main road and roll up the gravel driveway to a large mansion. A handful of ground floor windows shine with candle light, and a Butler or similar manservant stands trying not to shiver by the large front door.

Edgar passes the cab driver a couple of pound notes, and we step out into the cold evening. The house rears up menacingly in front of me. I have never seen a building so ill at ease. It sits rigid, uncomfortable amongst prickly ornamental shrubs and itchy close-shaved lawns.

I carry my backpack awkwardly over one shoulder, hoping I won't be creasing up my suit. My nerves jangle with each step, drawing up to the tall front door.

Was coming here the right thing to do?

Again a bothersome wasp of doubt begins to flit about my ears. I'm not alone, I remind myself. I have Edgar with me. He's a stout chap, not easily bothered, and is used to circulating in these moneyed up-draughts. There's nothing to fret over.

The servant at the door takes our coats and hats, showing us in. I think I preferred it outside. The old house is fusty, and the air is thick with ancient layers of dust, cigar fumes, and an ashy haze from several open fires.

Wide and bisected by a sweeping staircase, the entrance hall gives us the option of three open doors, through which the sound of plummy conversation and restrained laughter drifts.

"Would you tell Matriarch DeVeire that we come bearing gifts." Edgar announces, tucking his monocle away into a waistcoat pocket.

The Butler offers to take my bag, but I clutch onto it.

"Please, these are precious. I would like to give them to her Ladyship in person."

"Madame does not often attend the gatherings. She keeps herself occupied, in her private rooms. You will be unlikely to see her, and she will accept no visitors."

My heart sinks, butEdgar nudges me in the direction of an open door. There is socialising to be done.

"What about-" I start, but he gives me an imperceptible shake of his jowled head. He takes the bag from me, and slips it under a clothed table of lamps and photographs.

"Hidden here, it will be safe and easily accessible."

He winks.

What does he have in mind? Before I can ask, a room full of eyes turn upon us, and conversation falters. The assembled men and women are a mismatched collection of high foreheads, long noses, shiny shoes, military medals, curled moustaches, bonnets, old fashioned hoop skirts and fluttering fans.

The dimming in the conversational volume is only brief, but it is a canyon of space and time. I am assessed with excruciating rapidity, and dismissed. The long noses and high foreheads and curled moustaches turn away and resume their conversations. The hoop skirts and fluttering fans swish and fidget with increased vigour.

A side table is laid with decanters of whisky and brandy, soda, glasses, cigars, and a bowl of chipped ice. Edgar pours us both a small measure, and we tap our glasses together in a quiet cheers.

I am relieved that the oaf has not yet seen us. No doubt he will be lurking somewhere, and so long as there is a handy shield of gentlemen and ladies all around me, decorum insists that he do nothing but play the gracious host. Anything else would be a great embarrassment.

At least, that's what Edgar had told me in the taxi.

We take a turn about the room. Edgar introduces me to a few people he knows, or is casually acquainted with. A Lord and Lady, a widowed Duchess and a Baron and his mistress.

Edgar moves away to talk business with a tall man in a long coat, and so I find myself alone in the unexpected presence of a very odd couple who look to be nothing but cobwebs in clothes, grey and powdery like chalk dust; Mr & Mrs Refulgence Pity.

They hover in a dim corner, away from the others, and seem as out of place as I feel, so we converse for some time.

The conversation is inoffensive enough, and I make sure to keep the topics centred on mundane, everyday matters, so as not to give away my lowly status. I am here masquerading as a rich man.

My suit is complemented, and Mr Pity insists on taking the name and address of my tailor. Tremblay will no doubt enjoy working for such a distinguished client, should he ever choose to look him up.

Edgar excuses us, leading me by the arm around the room, talking in low tones. While I was engaged in formal conversation, he has been gathering intel from snippets of chatter around the room. Beloved Mother's rooms are on the third floor, on the far side of the house. She has been dressed for the party, but as the Butler stated, was unlikely to come down and socialise.

"All you need do is excuse yourself to the wash room, and head right up!"

I wait for a break in the conversation, where attention is mostly away from me, and slip from the room.

The servant has taken up his position outside once more, and so the entrance hall is clear. I remove my backpack from its hiding place, and hurry up the majestic sweep of the staircase.

The thick carpet underfoot hushes any sounds my feet might make, and as I scale the heights within the great

DeVeire house, the noise of the soiree diminishes. The solid floors and abundant soft furnishings absorb all sound.

The third floor is decorated in shades of deep red, lit by candles near the end of their lives. Corridors stretch left and right, and I wander left first. I listen at doors, hoping for some sign of occupation. I knock on one door, and push it open. It is a bedroom. Or, it had been a bedroom.

Dust sheets cover the furniture, a landscape of heavy muslin mountainsides. I am about to close the door and continue my search for Beloved Mother, but I felt the need to linger. The nearest dust sheet covers some kind of dressing table. Lumps and bumps below the fabric indicate there are still picture frames and grooming equipment out. Curiosity gets the better of me, and I take hold of the sheet, gently lifting it.

Male grooming paraphernalia litters the surface, and in the picture frames are grim looking family photos. Beloved Mother sits in a flowing black gown, beside which stands a man I take to be her late husband, and on either side of them stand two young men.

No more than boys, it is clear who they are. Lawrie and the oaf. Even as children they held themselves differently. The Dear Departed leans casually on the back of his mother's chair, while his older brother has his hands clasped tightly behind his back, scowling. I take up the picture and stare for a long time at it. Lawrie has his mother's gentle expression, and his father's strong jaw.

I have a matriarch to locate, and lingering here is not

helping me in this endeavour. I leave the room as I found it, and retrace my steps.

There are now muffled sounds coming from behind a door across the stairway, at the other end of this long corridor. I follow them, and tap upon the door. There is no acknowledgement of my knocking, and so I try the handle. The door is unlocked and it swings easily open.

Beloved Mother has her back to me in the middle of the room. She works at a tall table, dressing a small body.

She can't have a child, can she? I don't know of any DeVeires younger than Lawrence. I cough politely, and she shrieks. She spins around, clutching at her chest.

"Intruder!"

"I've come to return his things! Sorry, I didn't mean to scare you!" The words fall out of my mouth in a tangle.

I'm an idiot, I tell myself, I should have knocked louder. As introductions go, this is exactly the opposite of what I had hoped for.

Her rooms are vast. One entire wing of the great house is taken up by her private lodgings. A house within a house.

The first thing that I notice isn't the sparse furnishings, or the large portraits, or the plate of half-finished food on her table. No. What I notice first and foremost is the smell. Well, smells. There are a lot of them, all layered one atop another. Lavender and sweet rosewater overlays the moisture in the atmosphere, under which is the distinctive odour of dog piss.

Revealed upon the table is not a child as I had initially thought. It is a poodle, and it is half dressed in a smart green suit. She extends one gnarled and crooked finger toward me, her face a map of jostling creases.

"Look away!" Her voice is shrill and piercing, "Bitty is *indecent*!" She hides the partially clothed dog under a blanket, huffing and tutting irascibly.

A chorus greets me as I step forward into Mother DeVeire's private drawing room. Barking and chirping and cawing from her peculiar menagerie. Dogs and cats and birds of varying sizes fill the floor, sofas, and the tops of cabinets. In one corner, under a dim bulb a tortoise looks up at me lazily, blinking its watery eyes.

My initial surprise at this loud greeting is matched only by my surprise at seeing that every single animal is clothed. Tailored trousers and jackets are worn by the dogs, the cats are in knitted cover-alls, and the birds wear strange undergarments like a baby might. One particularly loud grey parrot also sports a bow tie.

I realise I have frozen to the spot and am now surrounded by small bouncing dogs, while suspicious felines pad softly in circles. I pick up one foot, moving it forward through the hairy maelstrom, careful not to step on any of them. Then the next.

It takes me a while, as the excited dogs refused to keep still, and continuously jump up at my side, sniffing and pawing at me.

Beloved Mother stands stiff as a broom. She watches

as I move through the room at the centre of a whirl of paws and fur and feathers. Her expression is pinched and fearful. She is deeply suspicious of my presence, snooping around her house.

"We dress ourselves so as not to be indecent," She indicates the animals, "As it should be for *all* of God's creatures."

"Forgive my surprising you," I breathe slowly, trying and failing to remain calm under the glare of her beady little eyes, "I have some of Lawrie's possessions. I've come to return them to you. I thought it the right thing to do."

I watch as the suspicion fades from her face. It is not gone, but calmed. She indicates a seat, and I move to it gladly, stumbling over the tails and paws of keen dogs and curious cats.

Beloved Mother waits for me to place my bottom on the uncomfortable cushion before she too moves to sit. One by one the noisy welcoming committee loses interest in me. Birds return to their cabinet perches, cats to their cushions, and the dogs to their snuffling and stretching and rolling about.

I can't take my eyes off of one dog in particular. A spaniel, which lays under its owner's chair. It doesn't look at all well, and I recall the disgusting doodle in her letter to Lawrie.

The letters.

My hands shake nervously as I fish them out of my backpack. I arrange them neatly, and hold them out. Beloved

Mother moves slowly, her hands taking the letters delicately. She is hesitant, unsure what it is I have given her. Upon recognising her own handwriting, she clutches the letters to her chest, eyes squeezed shut.

"He kept them." Her voice is hoarse, "Thank you."

Next I pull from my bag the remainder of the belongings I thought right and proper to return to the family. His books, some photographs, and a small number of his more expensive looking garments.

All of these things she hugs to her chest, burying her face in his clothes, "I can smell him, still." Blinking back tears, she reins in her emotions. Heaven forbid a Lady of her standing actually *feel* something, "Tell me," Her small dark eyes rest on me, heavy and penetrating, "Was he happy?"

My nerves are calmer now. I'm still on edge being in this woman's presence, but there is a new atmosphere between us. A weight is lifted, and I can speak more easily, without stuttering and spewing all my words.

"We were very happy."

"*We?*"

Oops.

Perhaps I have become a little too relaxed, and slipped up. I often forget myself, and speak as if everyone were au fait with the peculiarities of a queer life.

I sit up a little straighter, and remind myself to be more cautious, and also that we were never truly a couple.

A canary flutters onto my head, hopping in circles, pecking at my scalp. I wave it away.

"We shared a room in a lodging house. He was a close friend, Mrs DeVeire."

This satisfies his mother, and she begins to lay his artefacts onto a side table. She pauses before laying down the letters. Selecting a small number of them, she opens up the envelopes and scans them. She has selected the ones sent by his brother, and they obviously displease her.

She tuts, growing in irritation with every letter of his that she reads.

"Forgive me for asking, how did you know where he was staying? Did he ever write to you?"

One of the well dressed cats slips onto my lap, staring at me with intense green eyes.

Slapping down the letters, she checks her anger. Her jaw is clenching and relaxing, "That bloody boy." She glares at the envelopes, "I employed the services of a low sleuth to locate Lawrence. The information was to be passed on only to me." Angrily she taps a darkly painted fingernail upon the letters from Edward to his younger brother, "I shall have words with that shabby Mr Nettle!"

There it is. That word again. Nettle. It seems Oddly hadn't written in code. He referred to a man, hired to track down the wayward DeVeire!

Surprise is evident on my face, and Beloved Mother takes it as shock at her outburst. She relaxes her expression, attempting a motherly warmth, but coming up tepid.

"I apologise for my language. It has been a very trying time, of late."

I insist that she has no reason to apologise, and take one of her hands in both of mine. It is cold and fragile, the skin thin and I can feel the bones of her knuckles grinding against one another as she grasps at my fingers.

The physical contact seems to have an electric reaction. Her posture shifts. She grips my hand tightly, evidently starved of human contact since her husband died, and her son departed. Her creased lips crack into a smile, before she remembers herself, snatching back her limb and the sides of her mouth droop once again.

"That is a very fine suit." She says, changing the subject, "My little baby would look ever so lovely in one just like it." She ruffles the head of the sickly Spaniel.

"Thank you. Your friends Mr and Mrs Pity like it too. They even asked for the name of my tailor!"

At the mention of the guests, her head tilts to one side. Her lips tighten as she carefully considers her next words, "They spoke to you?"

"Yes. We had quite a long conversation."

"The Pity's are very particular about who they speak with. What is it, I wonder, about you?"

I shrug, reluctant to give anything away of myself.

"My father was *otherwise* as well, you know."

Beloved Mother moves away from me and to a large portrait. It is of a man with fiery eyes and wide nostrils. It is a melodramatic oil painting of Beloved Mother's beloved father, "He never mentioned it, of course. But I knew."

Otherwise?

Did she know that her son and I shared our lives, and each other's beds from time to time? Another cat decides to make a cushion of me. Did she know her son was gay?

"He too could see beyond the living." She says, casting me a pointed look over her shoulder.

Beyond the living?

Does she refer to *ghosts*?

Now I notice the brass plate on the lower edge of the frame, and the name it bears; Major Pimlico Pity. Pity? I must have looked as confused as I felt, as Beloved Mother glides in her wide hooped skirts to my side.

"I do not know what power it is that has urged you to me, but I thank you. And pass my thanks on to them, whosoever they might be." She claps her hands together, and the animals all start, alert and silent, "Bed Time!" She commands, and slowly, slightly reluctantly, they begin to slink and hop and skip from the room, "I think you have a soiree to enjoy."

Opening the door to her private rooms, she indicates that our time together has come to a close. I bow a little, and thank her, still thoroughly perplexed, and the door is closed in my face.

The corridor is dark. The candles have reached their ends, and sputtered out. I pause there for a moment, noticing a door that lays ajar further down the corridor, back toward Lawrie's sheeted bedroom. From within, gently dancing orange firelight can be seen.

Curious once again, I make my way to this door and

peer inside through the narrow opening.

The oaf! There is only some small items of furniture laying between me on the threshold and the open fire, so my line of sight is unhindered. He stands reading a book. But not just *any* book. It is one I recognise.

He finishes the last page, turning his nose up in disgust. He tosses it then into the fire, and I watch Lawrie's journal begin to smoulder. My attention has been so drawn to the fire, and the stolen item, that I don't notice Edward crossing the room and pulling open the door.

He walks into me, knocking me flat on my back. I kick my legs, shuffling away on the floor as fast as I can. He stares at me, recognition slowly dawning on his bulbous face.

"What are you doing here, *faggot*?"

"Nothing!" I lie, and pull myself up. He blocks my path to the stairs, and to his Mother's rooms. I'm trapped in a dead-end corridor with a man who I am sure would gladly floor me.

Edgar is too far away to be of assistance, and I am by no means a fighter. He moves forward, reaching out with meaty fists to take a hold of me.

"Edward? Why aren't you downstairs looking after our guests?" Beloved Mother has appeared at the doorway to her rooms. The light from within casts her as a motionless silhouette.

The oaf freezes, and his arms drop to his sides. The sound of his mother's voice renders him impotent. He turns and walks away, trotting obediently down the stairs. I move to thank the elderly widow DeVeire, but she retires and closes the door. There will be no second audience this evening.

The fire!

I dash through the door around which I was previously peeping, and to the hearth. It is a small grate, and the flames were poorly stoked, so the journal is not completely destroyed. I pluck it from the ashes and pat at it to kill the hungry embers, showering the carpet, and myself, with soot.

The hot sparks burn my fingers and stain my cuffs. I examine what remains. The thick leather cover and around a third of the pages are intact. I dust myself down as best I can, smooth my hair, and attempt to make myself smart and decent again. I need to find Edgar. There was more to the mystery of Lawrie's death revealed tonight than I could ever have imagined.

I have been looking for answers in the wrong place.

The Whisperers? A waste of time!

The clues were all here.

Edgar, puffing on a fat cigar, moves swiftly to my side when I return to the soiree, nodding into the far corner. He's letting me know of Edward DeVeire's presence.

"Yes. We had a little run-in upstairs." I say.

"You did?" Edgar is shocked, and notices the remains of soot upon my sleeves, "What the devil have you been up to?"

I wave the cadaver of Lawrie's journal at him, my back to the oaf, "He tossed it into a fire."

"What is it?"

Our hushed conversation stalls when Edgar spies Edward moving toward us. His face is set firm, haughty and superior. He stands beside us, looking everywhere but in our direction.

"I think perhaps the two of you have had quite your fill of the evening's entertainment, don't you?" He smiles and raises his glass to a passing Lady, "Your part in our lives is very much done."

"Are you sure about that?" I ask.

The question tumbles out of my mouth before I can stop it. Now he turns to face us, and for the briefest of moments I think he might strike me. There is a tension in his body; taught with muscles that I notice flexing under his shirt and jacket. Not only were his puffy ears acquired in a boxing ring, it seems that his width and stature is maintained in one still.

Edgar pours himself an extra large measure of Whisky, sipping it, making direct eye contact with the larger man, "We were extended the same invitation as everyone else here, so I think we'll stay and enjoy the remainder of the evening, thank you."

Despite the hot coals of Edward DeVeire's eyes burning in our direction for the following few hours, I can't deny that I actually enjoy myself.

It isn't my usual crowd, and I often fall silent, allowing Edgar to chat, laughing in the right places now and again.

I drink only one more measure, and eat a little of the delicate finger-food.

I attempt to engage Mr and Mrs Pity in conversation again, but they seem to have left early. When it comes to eleven O'Clock, we make our farewells and depart in a pre-booked taxicab.

"To the City Centre," Edgar shouts, patting the Cabby on the shoulder, "The night is young!"

On the journey into the City I enquire after Mr and Mrs Pity. Edgar confesses to knowing of no such family, and is perturbed when I won't be drawn on the reason for my enquiry.

Lady Nell sits on a stool at the end of the bar, chatting amiably with a handful of her regulars. When we arrive, she waves at us, calling us over. We hug and take another drink, which she offers on the house, before I began to re-count all that has happened over the course of the DeVeire soiree.

"You're drunk." Nell laughs at me.

True, I'm not a big drinker, and the little I have imbibed has mixed merrily with my excitement, making me giddy, "Why aren't you?"

"I'm working on it." She downs her short glass of gin, pulling a face.

I'm glad to see her up and about, but she moves less animatedly than usual. Her pretence of unflappable campery drops a little in our familiar company, and I see her wince once or twice. She remains in great pain.

Snatching a bottle from the bar, she slips slowly from her stool and into her private space. We follow.

Oddly lays in the foetal position, his breathing low, but more regular than it has been. Nell indicates the dilly boy with a wave of the bottle, "He seems in better form today, sure as eggs. I think he might make it back to the land of the living. And thank heavens that rancid canal smell has gone. It was putting me off my food!"

We arrange ourselves on crates and cushions and similar makeshift chairs, Edgar taking on the duties of Mother, filling our glasses. I will only be able to stomach a small amount of Nell's gin, but a large slug is poured into my glass. An Edgar measure.

"This does rather muddy the waters." Nell muses upon my revelations, "Still, we'll be able to get to the bottom of all this after next week."

She rolls her eyes and her head at my blank expression. But it dawns on me quickly. The seance!

"You've picked a date?"

"Now that the Ball is done you have my undivided attention in this phantasmagorical endeavour!"

Over another splash of gin we iron out the details. The place, the time, the date, the mirrors. There remains only one more thing; the additional person to make up our party.

"Leave that to me." I am slurring slightly, and so put aside the remainder of my drink, "I have an idea."

Edgar drops me off home in yet another Taxicab ride. I can hear him singing a saucy song as the car rattles away. His voice carries rather well.

I hurry up to my room where I snatch up some paper and a pen. First of all I write a note to Tiffin, detailing the specifics of the seance. Then I write a letter. I write it deliberately slowly, so as to make sure none of my inebriation makes it onto the page. It is sealed, a stamp is applied, and the address marked on the envelope.

Skipping down the stairs, I slide the note under Tiffin's door. Then I hurry into the street and around the corner to the nearest post box and slip the letter inside.

CHAPTER NINE

MIRRORS

"I'm already haunting you, isn't that enough? Now you want to summon me to be gawped at like a sideshow attraction?"

I wake up suddenly from a deep and empty sleep. My mouth is dry and there is sweat on my back. I sit up, and shake my head at the Dear Departed.

He stands leaning on the wall near the window, watching me. I can't tell if he's angry, or simply poking fun.

"What?"

"You've got a surprise party planned for me."

"I have?" I'm not awake yet, and I can feel a layer of yesterday's gin separating me from reality.

"The seance."

"Oh." My hangover allows my confusion and irritation to bubble quickly to the surface, "Well if you would answer a straight question, I wouldn't need to. You keep showing up, then popping off again as soon we start chatting."

He smiles at me, "You're adorable when you're angry." And he is gone.

I flop back onto my pillow, and will the pain behind my eyes to vanish just as miraculously.

Am I becoming accustomed to being haunted?

I have nothing to do today, and so I allow myself to slowly drift back to sleep, where I sink deeply into another black and empty, dreamless void.

The next week is torture, half expecting a reappearance from Lawrie at every moment. I hope for a reappearance. I want him to chastise me again. I want to talk to him.

Lady Nell's comment, so long ago it seems now of me 'fancying myself a Holmes' was rather prescient. I spend two afternoons making notes and plotting lines between names. I attempt to fit together the various pieces of the puzzle, but find myself at a loss.

I am not a Holmes. I'm barely a Watson. I'm just an untalented young man, disowned for his 'unnatural proclivities', as my Father had called them, barely keeping my belly full, if not for the kindness and generosity of friends. I wear out my little brain, like a hamster spending too long in its wheel.

I count down the days, and I count down the hours, and I count down the minutes until the seance. Such a turnaround from my initial reticence at putting on such an event! To say I am excited would be an understatement, but I am also very very nervous. I have received a reply to the letter I sent while tiddled, and reading it makes my stomach perform anxious summersaults.

"You're early." Saffron greets me warmly, sweeping me into an embrace once the front door of the townhouse is firmly shut.

The Library has been arranged as per instructions sent over by Madame Miasma earlier in the day. Saffron expresses how unimpressed she was by the lack of notice, but has obligingly organised the room to the mystic's exacting specifications all the same.

Five chairs face each other in a circle, behind which are positioned large upright mirrors, gathered from around the house or borrowed from neighbours. Surrounding this setup, the floor is laid with an almost complete ring of salt, and candles perch in elegant candelabras. She specified the room was to be lit only by candles. She specified *lots* of candles. And there are. As Edgar moves around the room, igniting the many wicks, the room becomes close with heat. In a very few minutes the room is stuffy and hot as an oven.

"This whole affair is rather amusing, isn't it, ducky?" Edgar confides, "Seems a silly exercise to me."

When Nell arrives, carrying a fresh bag of salt, she makes a great show of examining the room, and pointing out a tiny mark on one of the mirrors, which Saffron sets to with her sleeve at once, making it spik and span.

"You telephoned for more salt?"

I take the bag of fine white granules from Nell, and slowly lay a line of it across the floor, joining the two ends of the incomplete circle.

"This may just be a big show, a clever parlour trick," I admit, "But I happen to have seen a thing or two recently which tells me otherwise."

Edgar scoffs, but Nell glares daggers at him. He raises his hands in apology, then lights himself a cigar.

When Madame Miasma arrives, she looks markedly different to our last encounter. She looks somehow older, wizened, weary. She is dressed in a collection of black shawls and wraps, embroidered in pink, and with fringing that swishes silently as she moves.

The pungent aroma of sickly sweet perfumes that suffused her room follows her here, which does not go unnoticed by our gracious hosts. It is not a pleasant aroma.

I want to thank her for agreeing to perform this spiritual conjuring, but she holds a finger to her lips, and will not speak. She points at the chairs, and we take our seats.

Edgar, Saffron, Nell and myself make up four of the five participants needed.

"I rather think we're missing someone. Hiding with their tail between their legs?" Edgar chuckles mirthlessly, "Can't say I blame them."

Knock knock knock.

I shoot Edgar a smarmy grin before dashing off to answer the door. The recipient of my letter. The final participant.

I link her arm in mine, and we enter the Library.

Edgar's mouth hangs open, dropping the cigar that was resting there onto his lap, where a hot ember burns his crotch. He flails at it, putting out the spark.

Madame Miasma clicks her fingers to gather everyone's attention. She indicates that we should sit, and be silent. I lead the final guest to her chair, then move quickly to my own.

Beloved Mother looks around the circle with those penetrating dark eyes of hers, her expression unreadable.

From a cloth bag hidden somewhere amongst the

shawls and wraps, Miasma produces a tightly bound bundle of dried herbs. She ignites one end over a candle, then proceeds to waft it about the room. She covers every inch of floor space, waving the burning herbs high and low. I notice Edgar grow nervous as she waves the herbs near his books, but he needn't fear. She doesn't touch them. She barely looks at them. He relaxes as she moves away from his precious paperbacks.

Her focus is somewhere else. Not in the room. Her eyes dart about, as if searching for something beyond the power of sight. This continues for some time, until the air is thick with the heady aroma of sage and other unidentifiable spices. Her perfume lingers, the sweet and savoury scents mulling the air.

Now Miasma picks up a candle, and walks into the centre of the circle. In her other hand she holds a small silver bell. She stands motionless, closing her eyes, taking long deep breaths.

"Everyone must hold hands now." She affects a deep and peculiar voice, "I need silence and calm in which to push back the veil between this realm and the next. What you are about to see may cause you some alarm. Please, remain seated. Do not speak. Do not be afraid. I am in complete control."

She waits a while now, turning, looking us over one by one, the candle in her hand slowly releasing thin rivers of white wax over her knuckles.

To my right sits Edgar, his hand doughy and warm

in mine. To my left sits Nell, whose long fingers are thin and cold by comparison. I can feel the tension in their bodies through these gently grasping digits.

Edgar is watching Miasma, clearly dubious, while matching her breathing unconsciously.

Nell is impatient, her whole demeanour screams 'get on with it.'

I can hear my heartbeat in my ears, such is the lack of sound in the room; The slow pulse of the Medium's breathing an arrhythmic accompaniment to the percussion in my veins. My nervous excitement sets me on edge, and my ears strain for any noise, any hint of something supernatural.

I cast my gaze around the room, tearing my attention from Miasma's form for a moment, her head now bent low to her chest. Her breathing slows and becomes laboured.

I will for Lawrie to appear, and to smile at me, and toss his hair, laughing at how absurd this all is.

Miasma stops breathing.

Beloved Mother shifts uncomfortably in her chair, holding the hands of Saffron and Nell. Nell's loose grip tightens upon mine. Edgar grips me just as before, but I can feel his pulse quicken.

Miasma's head snaps up and she rings her little silver bell. The sound is like that of shattering glass in the dead of night. Bright, brittle and alarming.

Stepping forward, she makes her way swiftly toward Beloved Mother, holding the candle out in front of her. My attention has been so focussed on the Medium's meditation I hadn't noticed the odd difference in the mirrors.

Her reflections hold no candles.

Miasma holds the lit taper over Beloved Mother's head, passing it to her reflection in the mirror positioned there. Nell squeezes my hand tightly, her grip is strong, and Edgar stiffens. I fear both my hands will be bruised from their fingers digging into me.

"Lawrence Clifford DeVeire." The Medium intones, "There are friends, and family, who wish to speak with him. Find him."

Her reflection opens its mouth to reply, but bellows an unearthly howl instead of words. The howl alters and shifts, full of almost-words and half syllables, like a song heard underwater.

It is strangely familiar. The bathroom!

This is what I can hear when she's making those strange noises. Except it isn't her at all. It's her reflection!

The howling ends, and her reflection turns and walks away. In the mirrored Library it opens the door and is lost out of sight.

Lawrie's Mother hasn't seen the reflection at her back, only heard it, and her face has paled in surprise.

Tiffin takes up another candle.

All of her reflections are back, and once again I see that none of them hold candles. She moves this time toward Edgar, and passes the candle over his shoulder to the reflection at his back.

"Lawrence Clifford DeVeire. There are friends, and

family, who wish to speak with him. Find him."

Her reflection howls, once again an ear-splitting, toe-curling sound, then departs.

My heart rattles against my ribs. The heat and stuffy atmosphere of the Library makes it tricky to remain calm, and to hold my nerve.

I am aware a seance could be a spectacle, but I hadn't expected anything quite like this. Madame Miasma continues to pass candles into the mirrors, intoning the same command to send her reflections on their way.

The number of candles begins to dwindle as they are handed again and again into the mirrors, and into the hands of the reflections waiting there. The room grows colder, and the faint candle light now casts long shadows around the room. They criss cross, creating a wavering checkerboard of varying depths and darkness.

Miasma abruptly stops her repetitive ritual, when a distant howl reaches our ears. It is akin to nails down a blackboard, yet a fearful and wet sounding utterance.

Then another. And then another, each of them emitted from a different corner of the Library.

I catch the Medium's eye. She has been taken as much by surprise as us. Quickly she fetches handfuls of trinkets from her concealed bag, dropping them. Marbles and bones and feathers and playing cards.

She watches how they land, and squints her eyes, attempting to pull a meaning from the chaos. But these odds and ends do not keep still. They lift into the air, and move about. They rotate and drift, they swirl and flutter, as if caught in some incredible breeze.

Another howl, and then another, closer and closer.

All eyes are on Madame Miasma, as she turns about, shawls and wraps shimmying over her thin frame, as she tries to snatch her bits and bobs out of the air.

This is definitely not how the seance is meant to progress. I consider standing up, leaving my seat and helping her.

As if reading my mind she shakes a finger at me.

"Stay put!" Her usual voice has returned, pretences dropped, "The spirit of Lawrence can't be found. But there's something else..."

"What do you mean, *something else*?" Nell spits.

"He's being blocked, or he's refusing to appear, I'm not sure. It's not like there's a manual for the afterlife!"

Beloved Mother says nothing, but shoots me a brief and disappointing glance. She was as hopeful to see Lawrence tonight as I have been, and I've let her down. She will not see her son again, this poor grieving mother. Instead she has been witness to an evening of spooky otherworldly farce.

I am not sure how Tiffin has managed to trick us into seeing her miraculous mirror Miasmas. I give her ten out of ten for ingenuity.

The remaining candles gutter and struggle as a chill takes hold of the room. I feel it at my back, like a slab of ice has been pressed against it.

"Please help me." The voice is small.

It is that of a child.

I look about to locate the source of the voice. There is a presence at my shoulder, but when I turn I can see no one there.

"Did you hear that?" I ask, and everyone nods, now letting go of hands, breaking the circle.

Edgar raises a shaky digit, pointing past me, "There are children in my Library."

And indeed there are.

Moving out the deepest areas of crossing shadows children materialise. Some in rags, and clothes of bygone ages, others dressed more neatly. Not a one of their forms possess any colour. They look to be made of the same cobwebby, chalk dust material I noted in the clothes and faces of the Pity's.

But *they* had been real enough, hadn't they?

Tiffin is floundering. She begins to instruct her reflections to remove the children, but they can not. These spectres are not in the mirrored world, they are very much in ours.

"Keep back!" The Medium shouts, producing now a crucifix, waving it around to no effect, "You were not summoned. You are *uninvited*."

Watching the young ghosts spread out about the room, I realise they are maintaining their distance from us, all the while reaching out, begging us, imploring us to help them, to save them.

How? And from what?

Their voices burble and mingle, so that no one word can clearly be made out. It is a cacophony, steadily growing in volume. These must be poor lost souls, dead children cursed to roam the Earth, never finding peace.

The ring of salt holds them at bay.

The only one of us still seated is Beloved Mother, her old bones preventing her from leaping up in alarm. The nearest undead children call out to her, beg her, plead with her, tears running down their faces. She cannot look at them, and clutches at her own sleeves defensively.

With as level a head as she can manage, Saffron moves to the edge of our protected circle, "Tell me," She whispers to the children, "How can we help?" She extends a hand beyond the circle of salt, and one of the children snatches hold of it.

"No!" Tiffin screams.

But nothing happens.

Saffron holds the hand of the young girl who latches onto her, bringing her other up to stroke the pale face.

"They're just children."

My hair and clothes are tugged by an inexplicable wind, which kills the few remaining flames, knocking over the candles, and pushing us all into inky darkness, and a deafening silence.

The children become quiet, as fast as an electric light dims once turned off at the switch. My heart beats loudly in my chest, and I pant, listening. There is movement in the unseen, shuffling of feet and the rustling of fabric.

A match strikes and Edgar relights a candle. This tiny orb of golden light in the vast empty hollow of the Library does nothing but make the darkness all that much deeper. The children are gone, and the salt circle has been smeared like dunes across the floor, broken and irregular.

All eyes on Miasma, she remains mute, unsure of herself, dishevelled. Her mouth flaps like a fish stranded out of water, gasping for air and for understanding.

We decamp to the drawing room, where Edgar attempts to sound out the meaning of the eerie visitation. No logic can be found in it.

"Remarkable! Astounding!" He thunders, "I'm so sorry for doubting your vision, Rowan."

"As well you should be!" Nell ribs Edgar, "*I* saw him too you know. By the canal. Only briefly. But I have seen the ghost of Lawrie as well."

"But why! What brings him into being? What summons him? What sends him away?" Edgar puffs enthusiastically on his cigar.

"Stop your pacing and waffling, would you?" Tiffin sighs as Edgar's feet chart a course past her once again. She is slouching upon the settee in a most unladylike fashion, "There's no reason to be found in it. There's no set way the undead behave. They'll do what they want. All we can do is hope to channel the *right* spirit, and see what happens." She waves her hands dismissively in the air.

"These may be common or garden events for you,

but this is all rather new to me!" Edgar retorts hotly.

He is mightily unimpressed with her demeanour and lack of helpful insight.

"Those poor children." Saffron mutters distractedly, shaking her head, winding her dark hair around and around her fingers.

Beloved Mother, who has been observing us quietly since the seance ended now stands. Everyone becomes hushed, respectful, waiting to hear what it is she may wish to say on the matter.

She takes my arm, clearly wishing to have a private word. I walk her out of the room, and she steers us toward the front door.

"My father was part of a deeply spiritual family." Her dry voice rasps in her throat, quiet and pained, "Not religious. I mean spiritual in some other way, one that even I do not entirely comprehend."

"The portrait. It was titled Pimlico Pity. Are the Pity family somehow connected with ghosts and phantoms and the like?"

She nods, "I am a God fearing Catholic woman, raised in my Mother's faith. Strictly speaking I should not have attended this event."

"You're very naughty." I grin, and she cracks a rare and fleeting smile in reply.

"I have always known the world to hold more wonders than I might ever see in my time upon God's Earth." She pauses at the door, turning to me, "I was a fool to be so hopeful as to see my dear boy once again today. However what I witnessed confirms that whichever strange path you are on, it is one you must follow to its conclusion."

"Thank you for attending, Mrs DeVeire." I say to her, honestly and whole heartedly, "It means a great deal, for you to trust me."

I open the door and for a moment she pauses.

"Please, call me Narcissus." Then she is away, her long skirts disappearing into the foggy night.

The fact the Dear Departed didn't appear causes me some concern, but what is more bothersome is who did. All those tiny, pale, pleading, desperate faces flit through my thoughts at unwelcome moments, sending frequent icy shivers up my spine.

Edgar calls on me one evening, early the following week. The day has been dark and rain pours continually through the hole in the roof over the stairwell.

"Have you ever been to a Boxing match?" He asks, as he ushers me out into the street.

"No. Never. Why?"

"Cockfight?"

"Never!"

"Well It's like a Cockfight, except between people."

I pull my coat tightly around me, sheltering from the insistent rain with my new umbrella. Today I did not forget to wear my gloves, "I know what Boxing *is*. I just haven't been to a match. I'm not a fan of violence as entertainment."

"You're a delicate flower." He says, plucking the lavender from my lapel, tucking it into his pocket, "Just in case, eh? Don't want you ruffling anyone's feathers, do we?"

I doubt anyone attending a boxing match would know what the flower symbolises, and say as much, but Edgar laughs at me.

"It's not about symbolism. It's about appearances and bravado. Your common or garden masculinity shies away from the dainty and delicate, such as your little lavender."

I trust Edgar on this. He has had to put up such a front his entire life, whereas I have shied away from it, and found my own version of what it is to be 'a man'.

"I still don't understand *why* you're taking me to a Boxing match."

Edgar's face is grave, as he leads me this way and that down the dark alleys and ginnels that stretch, hidden, behind the imposing buildings of the City centre, "You will."

Through a door obscured by deliberately placed crates and containers, which opens up when Edgar gives his name to a man peering at him through a slit at eye level, we find ourselves in a cellar crammed with shouting, cheering men.

The centre of the room holds the ring, in which two topless men bare-knuckle fight. They are bloodied, and one man's eye is swollen so that it will not open. His one good eye is bloodshot. He spits onto the ground, bouncing on the balls of his feet, bandaged fists raised in front of his face. His opponent is a smaller, wiry man. He is all sinew and ropey limbs. Muscles ripple under his skin as he tenses and moves left and right, faking blows and dodging those from his battered competitor.

"I want to show you something." Edgar shouts into my ear, over the din of the spectators.

The press of bodies is a jostling, swarming mass of raised arms and stale cologne. Hungry looking, weasel faced men slink about the crowd, making notes in small black books, taking money thrust in their direction; taking bets.

The cheering and jeering doesn't quite cover the bone-crunching thuds of the blows as they land. I hear something crack, and the spry little chap is felled. A lucky left hook caught him off guard, and he has hit the floor. The crowd sags, moaning and shouting at the referee.

Edgar pushes me in front of him, steering me to a back corner, where we climb up onto a bench to get a better view. I must admit the charged energy of the room is a little infectious, making my heart beat faster, but the air tastes of blood and sweat, grounding my senses in the horrible nature of the spectacles witnessed here.

"We're just in time for the next match." Edgar points across the room, "The fighters will come up from a side room over there. You watch."

I wait as the prone body of the previous loser is carried away. The victor parades around the room, receiving congratulations from some, being harangued by others.

The next fighters emerge, once again shirtless and

with their knuckles bandaged for protection. One of the weasel-faced bookies announces them, and the betting opens.

The fighter that most people appear to be putting their money on is none other than Edward DeVeire.

We watch the fight, and I am mesmerised by the large man's savagery. His wide shoulders power thick arms, which move with incredible speed and accuracy. I would have thought him a slow and lumbering fighter, but am proven wrong by this display. His eyes burn with a manic intensity, and even when his opponent falls to the canvas, follows him down and continues the assault. The referee has to push his way between them to halt the pummelling.

I watch, agog. The savagery and unceasing onslaught of fists is a terrible and incredible sight to behold.

"When you went to see the Whisperers with Nell," Edgar asks me, "How *exactly* did they say Lawrie was killed?"

I can't peel my eyes from Edward DeVeire and those frantic, brutal fists. No longer a man, he is something more primal. His big chest heaves up and down as he takes deep gasping breaths, sweat glistening across his mottled and bruise-patterned skin. His mouth hangs open, teeth bared, a streak of blood across one cheek.

Standing there I see not a man, but a beast.

The winning gamblers collect their money as Edward, degree by minute degree regains his restraint, and once again shrugs on the persona of a Gentleman.

We linger at the rear of the room. I am fearful we will be seen, and so plead with Edgar for us to depart. I keep an eye on the oaf, as he begins speaking to someone in the crowd. This new man has a thin nose, wide head and only a few strands of hair. I catch his eye, and he says something to Edward. The two of them turn in our direction.

"Yes," Edgar finally agrees, "It is about time we wagged our flippers. Let's scarper." He pushes me toward the exit, and I employ elbows to forge a path through the crowd at a swift pace.

At the door I pause, turning to see if we are being pursued. Thankfully we are not. Edward and this other man exchange words, their eyes fixed in our direction until the press of bodies closes between us.

The door opens and we launch ourselves into the rain, and away down the alley.

We are halted on our journey back across the City by a Police whistle. We duck into a doorway, fearing the worst, finally able to breathe easy when we realise the sound is not connected to our presence.

My nerves are on edge, Edward's eyes peer at me from a corner of my imagination.

We are near the entrance to the Canal where Lawrie had appeared to Nell and myself. A Rozzer is struggling to carry something up the stairs from the side of the water to street level.

I move forward to lend a hand, but Edgar pulls me back, "Don't get involved." He hisses.

Huddled there in the dark doorway, I begin to connect some dots, "How did you know he'd be fighting?" I ask Edgar.

"I know people who know people. A man in my position wouldn't get very far in life without connections." He winks at me, which seems pointless in the dark.

"You and Nell have been talking?"

He nods, "She told me what was said, but not who said it. I thought maybe we should see his fists in action. Just a hunch."

Running feet meet my ears, and two Bobbies clatter to a halt at the steps. Between the three of them they haul the lank and wet lump onto the pavement. They lay it out, and push back the blood soaked fabric that covers it.

Pasternak's lifeless face stares at the night sky, thick raindrops bouncing off of her wide eyes, and into her open mouth, ringed with lips discoloured to a deep, cold, blue.

"It's the old crone who told us Oddly had been attacked." I whisper, "After Lawrie it was Oddly, now Pasternak..."

Edgar pulls me back further into the shadowy doorway as one of the officers moves away, blowing his whistle for assistance.

"We need to warn Tremblay. He's next in the chain."

While backs are turned, we slip from our hiding place and hurry away. The Tailor's shop will not be open until morning, so we retire to Nell's Place to gather our wits.

"You think the *oaf* killed them?" Nell spits her gin at me accidentally.

"Yes. Maybe. I don't know, I'm tired. But he does have *something* to do with it!" My brain is far from the lean thinking machine of Holmes, and I can't quite fit all the pieces together, "The journal, what Tremblay said about how Lawrie died, this Nettle character..." I scratch my head and sigh, "I wish Lawrie would just tell me what's going on!"

Edgar harrumphs, "Well if that Miasma had been any good, we might have some answers. But no, I got a Library full of dead children instead!" He looks exhausted, and rubs his eyes, "I've not been sleeping too well. Sat up wide eyed like an owl all the way through the night."

"They really did wobble your jelly, didn't they, those little spooks?" Nell shoots Edgar a disbelieving glance.

He grumbles, "They're still there. They didn't leave. Now and again I can hear them, all around the house, chattering like tits in a hedgerow. And no matter how much I stoke the fires, the house will not be warmed."

I offer for Edgar to take what was Lawrie's bed, but he refuses, insisting that leaving Saffron alone for the night would be unthinkable.

We leave soon after, each to our own abode, with Nell promising to pay Tremblay a visit first thing in the morning.

CHAPTER TEN

MR NETTLE

"You've a Lady caller." Mrs Taffeta has let herself into my room, and is nudging me awake. I wipe drool from my cheek and mumble something incoherent.

"Get dressed." She pokes me with a worn talon.

Dragging her slippers across the floorboards with tired feet, Mrs Taffeta hastens from the room, closing the door.

It is still dark, and as I look at my wristwatch I am surprised to find that it is barely 5am. Who would be calling for me at this time? I worry that perhaps Nell has come with news of Tremblay, so jump clumsily into my dressing gown and scurry barefoot down the stairs.

To my surprise I find Saffron waiting fretfully in the entrance hall. Her hair is a mess and her eyes are red and puffy from crying. My mind is still catching up with me, sleep still crusting my eyes. She runs to me and I hold her, squeezing her tightly as she is wracked with sobs.

"They've taken Edgar!" She manages to say, her words broken and strained.

"Who have?"

"They came in the middle of the night. The house is turned upside down. They took his books too."

I call for Mrs Taffeta, and ask her to put the kettle on. I need a cup of tea to fire up my brain, and as a balm for Saffron's distress.

We are permitted into the Landlady's private sitting room, where Saffron begins to manage her weeping, clutching hold of my hands, fearful to let go.

"What happened?" I ask, once I have my first sip of sweet warm tea, "Tell me again. Take your time."

Mrs Taffeta listens eagerly from the doorway sucking on a thin cigarette, hungry for gossip and intrigue.

"In the middle of the night. Edgar could not sleep and was reading in the Library. I heard the shouting and crashing. I thought we were being burgled."

"Who was it?" I imagine the oaf and his boxing chums, riled up from the evening of violence and beer, looking to continue their bloody sport; smashing and breaking their way into the Townhouse, "Did you telephone the Police?"

"*Dios mio*! It was the Police who took him away!"

Saffron sleeps curled up on Mrs Taffeta's settee. The stress and shock prove a powerful drain on her, so she slumbers deeply, her hands and feet twitching now and again as she dreams. I make a quick call to Nell on Mrs Taffeta's telephone, and another to book a TaxiCab for the morning.

Saffron sits tight against my side in the car as we speed toward her home. As we pull up we find the scene a peaceful one. There are no Police officers to be seen, and outwardly, nothing appears disturbed.

When we arrive at the front door however, we can see that the lock has been smashed in, and dirty boot prints mark the step. I think Saffron might be reluctant to reenter the house, but she strides ahead of me, throwing open the door.

Her shoes strike hard and loud on the floor as she inspects her home, and the damage done to it. Tables and chairs are tossed on their sides, lamps and vases smashed, pot plants and their soil strewn across the floor.

In the Dining room the gorgeous paintings have been slashed or pulled from the walls, and a great many books are missing from Edgar's Library.

"The whole house is like this." Saffron has made a thorough inspection, and her shoulders sag, "I have never been without my Edgar."

Removing my jacket I roll up my shirt sleeves.

"Come on," I say, attempting resolve and comfort and strength, "I'll help you get tidied up."

She squeezes my hands in thanks, and we begin to set right the mess in the Library. In a quiet pause, we both start at the sound of scraping and the tinkling of china elsewhere in the building.

Is there someone else here with us? I didn't hear anyone arrive. Could they have already been here? Hiding?

I pick up a candelabra and hold it out in front of me as a shield, making my way into the entrance hall.

The sound is coming from the dining room, and we pad softly toward the door. Together, we push into the room, prepared to find an opportunistic burglar, or a constable left on duty.

What we find is an immaculate room.

The destruction which had lain across the scene only a few minutes before appears to be undone. At least, mostly.

The broken and smashed crockery is gone, the furniture neatly in its place, and the pictures hung upon the walls once more.

"Look." I say softly, pointing to the floor.

Amongst the faint traces of dust and dirt that linger there are a number of footprints, in varying sizes, but all small. Children's footprints!

"They weren't there before."

The scraping and shifting sounds begin again, this time from the drawing room. We run across the hall and fling open the door. The room has been set right. Traces of soil on the floor and some scuffs on the furniture remain, but otherwise it is immaculate.

"The children?" Saffron asks, casting me a puzzled expression.

I laugh involuntarily, incomprehensibly, "It seems your ghosts are more useful than mine."

Slowly, and all the while unseen, the spectral children help to put the house back into some kind of order. Saffron's mood improves, until the morning edition of the Paper arrives. The headline drops the floor from my stomach, and Saffron's hands shake as she reads.

PRESUMED DEAD, WOMAN LIVES AS BROTHER FOR DECADES!

According to the article, the Police received a tip-off from a reliable source that Edgar Burrows was not who he claimed to be. This led to the raid on his home, and the revealing of his true identity.

Edgar had been born Rose.

This revelation is not news to me, or to those closest to him.

His parents were distant and uncaring toward their young children, born out of wedlock, and as the result of an affair, said some. The unaffectionate Burrows parents were cold and resentful, especially toward their young daughter.

So when her sickly twin brother passed away, a young household maid assisted the young girl, her secret lover, into switching identities.

She paid off a mortuary friend to keep their secret and ever since, Rose wore the identity of Edgar. It gave him more freedom, more power and control over his life, enabling him and Saffron to enjoy a happy and comfortable existence, even if they did have to do much of it in secret. He lived as a man for the freedoms it afforded.

"There is no way the Rozzers could have known this! No one would ever tell! It's unthinkable!"

The mortician passed away many years ago, and none of us would ever speak of it.

Amongst the article is a handful of quotes from shocked acquaintances and business partners. They certainly worked fast to put this story together for the morning print.

The first of these quotes is from Edward DeVeire.

The journal!

The Dear Departed must have written about Edgar in his blasted journal.

Saffron rips up the Paper in a fury, tossing the shreds into a bin, cursing loudly in her native tongue.

The two of them had always been so kind to me, so supportive and giving, I know that I somehow need to repay them.

"Shall we visit him? If they will allow visitors, we will make sure he's well."

The Desk Sergeant I spoke with during my previous visit is on duty when we arrive at the Station. Saffron insists on seeing Edgar under the pretence of being a Housekeeper checking on her employer.

The Desk Sergent sighs sympathetically, hurrying us through to the cells, "You have five minutes." He says, "Be quick."

We slip into the segmented recesses of the building.

There are separate cells for women prisoners, and it is into one of these cubes of brick and iron our friend has been locked.

He has been dressed in a stained and scratchy nightie like an old potato sack, and is curled up on a narrow wooden bench, the only piece of furniture in the cell.

He is not alone. There are women standing or slouching all around this small space. Street walkers and pickpockets, women snatched by the fist of the law for other minor offences, all attempting to avoid looking or talking to one another.

Edgar's craggy face lifts when he sees us, and rises from the bench. He winces, doubling over, clutching at his belly.

"Are you hurt?" Saffron reaches in past the bars to him, and he smiles through his discomfort.

"Nothing this old Mare can't handle." He says, moving closer, taking Saffron's hand in his.

From a distance an officer is watching, and so I position myself between him and the reunited couple, blocking his view, so that they may kiss.

"You shouldn't have come." Edgar says, glancing quickly to the distant observer, "It isn't safe."

He winces again as he moves, clutching his stomach.

"What did they do to you?" I ask, "Do we need to fetch a Doctor?"

Edgar shakes his head, "The bastards would never allow a physician in. Had their own pig-fisted staff surgeon in to take a gander at me."

I look down, and see a dark staining on Edgar's inner thighs, "Are you bleeding?"

"I was. Stopped now. As I say; pig-fisted."

The watchful Constable begins to stroll meaningfully in our direction.

"What can we do?" I ask urgently, "To get you out of here? Haven't you got a contact?"

"Wouldn't do any good. It's in all the papers from what I hear. Nell will be upset that I've managed a bigger scandal than she could ever hope for."

"I don't know about that." I smirk, trying to keep the conversation light and friendly, "What can we do?"

Saffron's big eyes are wet with tears, and she risks bursting out sobbing again. Her hands shake. Seeing her love in such a state of distress, pained, and physically abused has broken her resolve.

Edgar winks at me, "The papers love a scandal. Maybe they need a bigger story, and we might just have one for them, eh?"

The Constable rattles his baton against the bars of the cell, "That's enough now." He commands.

Saffron mouths 'I love you' to Edgar as we are ushered briskly from the cells and from the Station.

I spend the remainder of the day with Saffron at the town house. I feel rather useless, as I can't offer the support she needs. I'm no Edgar. She appreciates my efforts all the same, and I think she is grateful for the company.

The young spectres do not make themselves known to us, and I wonder what unusual children they must have been in life, to actively *want* to tidy up.

I am dismissed as the dark of evening spills across the sky. Saffron refuses to allow me to remain any longer. She is a proud woman, and feels she has imposed on me quite enough.

"You know where I am if you need anything." I say as I leave, and she kisses me on both cheeks.

I decide to take a walk, once back in the City Centre. I stroll from Piccadilly toward the canal, my feet leading the way automatically toward Nell's Place. I deviate and take myself off down side streets and unfrequented avenues. I need space to think.

All around me the night time landscape of the city shifts as people move in and out of shadows, as curtains are drawn on high windows, as lamps are lit in the doorways of nocturnal establishments, and as a silvery mist coalesces in the air. A silhouette beneath a street lamp up ahead catches my attention. It waves at me, then hurries away.

Who was that?

I move to the spot upon which the shadow stood. It is uncommonly cold here, cooler than it is outside of the lamplight.

Behind me I hear familiar laughter, and I spin around to catch a glimpse of the shadow again, further along the road now, leaning casually against a street lamp.

It is the Dear Departed.

I hurry on, but once again he winks out of sight. Gone. What phantasmagorical game is he playing with me? I hurry to where he was stood only a moment before, but he is nowhere to be seen once again.

To the side of me I hear water lapping, and notice the steps to the canal where he appeared to Nell. I descend the slippery stone stairway to the water's edge, and peer into the darkness which swallows the canal.

"Come along!" Lawrie calls to me from within the

tunnel, but I cannot see him, "This way, quickly. I haven't got long."

Not waiting to be told twice, I hurry into the darkness. His hand slips into mine, cold, but comforting. He pulls me onward into the darkness, and when I ask why we are here, he shushes me. I trip, and stumble, but he laughs and pulls me on.

The darkness is thick, almost solid, and plays tricks on my eyes. Now and again I catch a glimpse of the rippling surface of the water, or the brick wall at my side, but I can not see Lawrie.

After several minutes he stops dragging me, and presses me into a recess in the wall. I fall back against the cold bricks and he pushes himself upon me. I am stood tight against the damp stone and crumbling mortar, with every familiar curve and enticing bulge of Lawrie's body tantalisingly close to mine. He feels solid, alive, vital.

His hands rest on my chest, his crotch nudging mine, and his lips brush my cheek. They tingle, a static charge crackling between us. I reach out, taking hold of him around his trim waist, gripping tightly, pulling him closer.

We kiss.

I never thought a kiss could be so powerful, or last so long, or be so passionate. It is breathy and hot and wet and it sends my heart into a flurry. I am kissing a ghost, yet it feels the most natural and normal thing in the world. I am kissing the man I love.

I reach to undo my trousers, passion urging me on,

releasing my blood charged cock; eager, flushed, joyous. But Lawrie moves away. I reach out to grab him, my hands closing on thin air.

He is gone.

I open my mouth to call out his name, but raised voices alert me to other people nearby, and I hold my tongue.

My trousers slide down to my knees, and I am alarmed to find myself exposed. Hurriedly, but carefully, I tuck away my engorged cock, buttoning up my fly with cold and unwieldy fingers. I chide myself for getting so carried away in a public place, but my heart leaps with the thought when next Lawrie appears we can continue where we left off.

My eyes, now adjusting to the darkness can make out two men further along the tunnel. I peer at them, straining my ears through the echoes to catch their words.

"No, Mr Nettle, please! I've told you everything!"

That name! That man! He's here!

But who is pleading with him so pitifully?

I edge quietly in their direction, my back hugging close to the wall, my footfalls muffled by their voices, and by their movement over the cobblestones.

"That so? They're getting close, and Mr DeVeire wants no loose ends." Mr Nettle's voice is reedy and thin, and as he turns I catch a decent look at his face.

A thin nose, wide head and eyes like lumps of coal. It is the man from the boxing match. He carries a knife, and it is dangerously close to the neck of the man with which he speaks.

I must beware the Nettle's sting, and am mindful that I do not want to end up skewered on the pointy end of the glinting instrument.

The man cowering and pleading with Mr Nettle I can now see. It is the whimpering Doctor Mandelbaum.

"*I'm* not a loose end!" He is crying, "I can keep quiet! I can help you to get rid of the others."

"You've a tongue made for flapping." Mr Nettle sneers.

"That Oddly boy has survived!"

Mr Nettle takes this information in slowly. His eyebrows knit together as he moves the knife closer to Mandelbaum's Adams's apple, "Go on." He hisses.

"He was fished out of the canal. Got him stashed away, recovering."

"That is surprising."

"I've been treating him."

"Idiot!" Mr Nettle spits, pushing the Doctor roughly on the shoulder, knocking him back several paces. He stumbles, falling onto his back. The charcoal eyes burn down over the simpering Whisperer, "Why would you *heal* him?"

"It'd be suspicious if I didn't! But I can help you."

"Oh yes?" Mr Nettle is dubious.

"I can administer a tincture which will poison the boy. Undetectable. They trust me. *Please*, I don't want to die! Think of my wife!"

"You should be the one to think of your wife, *faggot*." Mr Nettle sheaths his knife, "You have one week. If he's not dead by then, we'll be going to the papers about your sordid double life, and your *dirty* habits." He spits the word dirty, as if the very word leaves a bitter taste upon his tongue.

Mandelbaum has sold us out.

He is being blackmailed, but he's one of *us*. He could have told someone, anyone, and we could have been helping him out of this situation. Instead he's sinking in deeper, agreeing to commit murder!

The passion of my recent encounter pivots toward the heat of anger. My hands shake and my heart beats in a fury, and in fear. My head tells me to remain calm, to wait in the shadows, to take this information to Nell. My heart rails in the opposite direction, insisting my fists bunch up and my jaw clench, ready to pounce.

And I pounce.

Tripping over my own feet I lurch forward, and miss striking Mr Nettle as I had intended.

My anger breaks as my actions catch up with me.

I barrel into him, connecting with the centre of his torso, and we both tumble sideways. I yell as I meet the floor, and hear an almighty splash.

Mandelbaum wails and shrieks, flailing his arms defensively in the air over his head. I turn this way and that, pushing up onto my knees.

Mr Nettle is in the canal. The velocity of my attack forced him well under the surface, and now he rises, spitting and cursing, flapping his arms in an attempt at swimming.

Mandelbaum whimpers, skittering like a terrified mouse away down the tunnel. He runs for his life.

I don't wait to see if Mr Nettle makes it to the canal side. Instead I make quickly after the sound of the little Doctor's beating shoes.

I break from the black of the tunnel and into the grey swirling mist, sprinting up the stone steps and across the street. But then I jog and slow, and walk then stop.

I listen.

Mandelbaum is faster than he looks, and has taken off, vanished into the tangle of Manchester's streets and alleys. Uncharacteristically, I curse. Nell's place isn't too far away, and I hurry there.

She is elsewhere, so I leave instructions with the bar tender that Mandelbaum is not to treat Oddly. I make him promise, and insist that he tells Nell what I have told him as soon as she returns. Again he promises, and I leave, mollified. Oddly remains safe.

Back in my little room, I dwell on my visit to Edgar, and his words to us; The Press love a scandal.

Sensation sells.

It is late, but I rouse Mrs Taffeta.

"Please may I use your telephone?"

She smells of alcohol, peering at me through wavering eyes and sneers, teeth stained purple by red wine, "I don't think so." She slurs, wagging a skeletal finger under my nose.

"It is of vital importance. There's been a scandal, you see. I must call the Papers. They have to know!"

Her posture changes as she steadies herself against the door frame. It takes her a moment to process my words, whereupon she blinks rapidly, leaning forward.

I trust that her ears, always eager for gossip, will persuade her brain to let me in, and grant me access to the telephone that lays there.

After a pause in which I worry she has fallen asleep while standing, she retreats, beckoning for me to follow.

I am connected with the Paper quickly, and despite the late hour am greeted by a friendly voice. I stutter and stumble over the story at first.

"Take your time." The voice on the other end of the line is warm and friendly, clearly used to frantic callers at all hours, "Just stick to the facts and take it easy."

Trying again, I recount events of recent weeks, and my suspicions. On the other end of the line I can hear the scratch of a pen, and now and again there comes an 'ooh' or an 'aahh' and occasionally an 'oh my' as the details unfold.

Mrs Taffeta sparks up another cigarette from the crushed stump of a previous pungent white roll-up. Listening. Keen. Sliding down the wall where she leans.

I hang up the telephone as my Landlady hits the floor, cursing loudly. I help her up and plonk her into one of her lumpily padded chairs. She tries to smoke the wrong end of her rollie, curls up, then begins to snore.

"What *is* all the commotion?" Tiffin demands as I pass her room, "Oh. It's you."

"Hello." I am tired, and in no mood to entertain this young woman. She stands there in her night clothes, still caked in an inch of makeup. The overpowering odour of her perfume drifts into the hall, giving her a hazy, incense infused aura.

I continue up to my room, and as I reach the top step realise I have been followed, "Do you want something?"

"Someone's tetchy." She stands with hands on her hips, "Just thought I'd offer my services again."

On the threshold of my room I linger, turning this offer over for the positive and negative possibilities, "Another seance?" I ask, "What makes you think it'd be any less of a failure than the first attempt?"

"Nothing. It might be a pointless endeavour. But I have an idea." She stares at me through those lashes like spider legs, "So are you going to invite me in or not?"

She doesn't bother to set a scene with chairs or mirrors or rings of salt, she doesn't bother with the deep and mystical false accent, and doesn't bother to hide her shock at the small dimensions and poor state of my room.

She sits herself as daintily as she can manage on the edge of Lawrie's bed. She looks youthful again today, and I wonder if she had affected the appearance of advanced years with makeup and trickery for the seance.

"I'm a Witch, you see." She says to me, continuing a conversation disjointed by my becoming lost in thought,

"Not really a Medium. And no I don't ride a broom, before you ask. Well, I have once. I might tell you about that one day, if you're lucky." She pauses to observe my reaction before continuing, "My expertise lay in the area of death and the undead. The tissue that holds those two realms together. The veil. The waiting room before the afterlife. Purgatory. However you want to phrase it."

"I see." Nothing is a surprise to me now. Whether Tiffin is a Witch or not doesn't matter one jot. What does matter is if she can make her talents useful, "So how do we contact Lawrie? Why didn't it work?"

She shakes her head, "I don't know. It's not a *science*. There is no precise formula. But where a large summoning with lots of energy failed, a smaller, more intimate, more *personal* approach might win out." Casting her eyes around the room, she takes in the few items of furniture, and the fewer possessions on display, "We need something belonging to the deceased. Something *personal*."

I have just the thing.

Handing it to Tiffin, I warn her to be careful. She takes hold of it tightly in both hands, "Oh yes!" She says, grinning, "Ideal." She examines the charred journal with fascinated eyes, "You are his anchor. I can feel it, through this book. Incredible."

She closes her eyes, latching her lashes tight, clutching the journal close to her chest. Flakes of ashy paper are schlepped free in her embrace, cascading down her lacy night dress. I worry that she will damage it further, and reach forward to warn her, when her eyes snap open, and a deep chill takes hold of the room.

Creaking frost erupts across the walls, fractal patterns spreading like flowers into the air. I feel dizzy, and I steady myself using the wall. I can't focus, my sight is tinged blue, and strange angular shapes emerge around me, rotating, undulating. I am inside a kaleidoscope, and I feel queasy.

Within this confusion visions leap out at me. They are places and people I have never seen before. Hands that aren't mine reach out, feet that aren't mine run beneath me, a face that isn't mine looks back at me from a mirror. I am walking in the footsteps of the Dear Departed.

My stomach drops, I am travelling at speed. Spinning. I am falling. Tiffin catches me, concern written large across her face.

"Did you see that?" She asks.

I nod, "I think so. I saw something. I'm not sure."

"They were his memories. Are you well enough to try again? Sit down this time."

I make myself comfortable in the armchair, playing with some loose strands of the crocheted throw.

Tiffin clutches the journal tightly to her chest once again, eyes open this time, staring into mine.

"We need to focus. Just then, that was like diving into the middle of the ocean during a storm, after only one swimming lesson. We need to wade in slowly, from the beach. Get our toes wet. You understand?"

I say I do, though I have no clue as to how to progress any differently into the Dear Departed's memories than I did only a minute ago.

Tiffin's form diminishes as a dizziness sweeps over me. The room blooms in frost and ice once again, but slower, more delicately than before. Furniture and the walls and the floor break into fragments, swirling, kaleidoscopic.

I hear Tiffin's voice, calm and quiet, guiding me. I can't identify any words, her voice seems as broken into pieces as the world around me.

I am spinning.

I am turning, swept sideways in this sharply edged, ice-blue hurricane. I grip the arm rests, swaying and pitching like a ship at sea.

I see through Lawrie's eyes. He sees me, and I feel the warmth of his affection. At the same time I feel his desire to keep me at a distance, to protect me. He believes our time together will be over too soon, and does not wish to upset me.

I swing around, and now I see him speaking with a large woman in a ruffled dress and feathers in her hair. She is cross with him. I recognise the street they are on, and understand who this woman is.

Spinning in a new direction, another memory sinks through the silt of my consciousness. He is speaking with Oddly, preparing... Preparing to go away.

Upside down and round and around I flip, as memories begin tumbling faster and faster into my head. Then there is panic.

Running. Feet hurting from running so fast.

Pulling up short, down a dark alley. Blocked.

'Come home.' A voice commands, 'Let's have no more of this stupidity.'

Edward DeVeire steps from the shadows toward me. Toward Lawrie.

Angles are all askew, up is left and right is grey and colour is darkness. Edward blocks our egress from this alley.

There is another man. A man with a knife. Mr Nettle.

'Do as your brother says. It's for the best. Think of your poor mother.'

We shake our heads. No. We have a new life now.

We know love now. We don't want to give that up. We try to flee. Edward takes hold of us, and we hit him. A fist to the face, and it shocks him.

His expression twists, bestial. Before our eyes he changes. A vile metamorphosis. He becomes the monster of the Boxing ring, and we are struck.   Falling back, winded, I can't breathe. Lawrie can't breathe. I bring up my hands defensively as Edward lands fists upon my body. My ribs crack, my head bounces off of the floor, grit stuck into my cheek.

He doesn't stop.

'Enough! The poor lad's had enough!' Mr Nettle pulls at Edward, but he does not listen.

Then it is dark, and time has passed. Another hand upon us now, a kinder hand, a softer hand. Oddly is with us as we struggle to breathe, struggle to move.

'Don't tell Rowan.' We say, 'Keep him safe. I don't want him upset.'

And then we die.

I gasp for air like a drowning man as I surface once more in my dingy little room, and find myself confronted by the wide staring eyes of Angelica Tiffin. It takes me a few minutes to come to my senses, and to slow my heart and my frantic gasps for air.

"Did you see that too?" I ask, and she nods.

I can feel the ache in my bones from the beating, and there is a pain in my chest. Lawrie had thought of me in his final moments. Tears well in my eyes, and I try to push the vision of Edward away from my thoughts, but he looms there, a vast and bulging shadow, red eyes flare like sparks, and he brandishes fists hard and gnarled as boulders.

I am drained, and upset, and want to be alone. I thank Tiffin, and show her out. Curling up then in Lawrie's bed, I clutch the remains of his Journal.

"Why couldn't you simply have told me what happened to you?" I don't know if he can hear me, or if he is even near me right now, "Instead of leaving me to witness it for myself."

His arm reaches around from behind me, and holds my chest tenderly. He presses himself against my back, kissing the nape of my neck. His presence is a comfort, yet it also prises open the aching pit in my heart that cracked open when he died.

I hold his hand, and allow my tears to flow. We lay there, entwined, silent, as I drift off to sleep.

CHAPTER ELEVEN

A SITTING DUCKY

"Who was that woman?" Tiffin asks, barging into my room the next morning.

Woman? Oh yes. The angry woman from the vision.

"She runs a brothel not far from here. Why?"

I have been up and dressed for hours. I slept deeply, but briefly. When I woke the Dear Departed was no longer with me, and I was in my own bed, tucked snuggly under the covers.

Tiffin shrugs, "No reason. Just curious."

"If you're still feeling as generous with your talents as you were yesterday, I have a favour to ask."

The shock of last night's vision has given me a divine clarity. An idea, conjured from the melting pot of my memories has bubbled to life, formed shape and is beginning to solidify.

Tiffin folds her arms, "Is that so?"

I have a plan, a scheme, a way for Lawrie to see justice, and I tell her as much of it as I have fully formed at the current time. It is not much more than an outline that I give, but she is amused enough by it to agree.

"Do you think you can manage your part?" I ask. Her hit and miss performances do not instil a great deal of confidence, yet I am hopeful.

"Of course!" She takes offence at my tone, "Consider it done!"

We agree on a timeframe and her course of action. As Tiffin leaves, I wonder if she really has ridden on a broomstick like a Witch in a fairy tale, or if she said that simply for effect.

I have lots to arrange, and as I open the front door I am greeted by a raised fist. I flinch involuntarily, before I realise it has been raised simply to knock.

"Hullo." Says a small man with bright eyes and very pink skin, "I was wondering if you can help? I'm looking for Rowan Forrester."

Before I admit to being myself I ask for this man's name and credentials. He presents his business card.

"Irving Periwinkle. You're Mr Forrester aren't you?" He looks me up and down quickly, "I took your call last night." He reaches to his lapel, folding it forward and revealing a sprig of lavender hidden there.

"You've come to get the full story?"

"Something like that."

I am reluctant to waste too much time in telling him the same story I gave over the telephone only a few hours ago, "Accompany me?" I ask, "I have some errands to run."

As we walk and talk, Irving reveals that the journalists dismissed my story as fantasy, ridiculous, or were fearful of touching it, given the reputation of the DeVeire family.

"I'm new at the Paper you see. Not much more than a dogsbody. But I've had my work in print now and again. Token jobs for the most part."

"You want to write up my story?"

"It's fantastical. It's ridiculous, and it's horrible. And anyone who would murder their own kin needs taking to heel."

"Will you include the more... esoteric... elements of the story?"

Irving shakes his head, "I want it to be credible. No one will believe it if I also write about hauntings and such-like."

I had gone a little overboard on the telephone. Even as I had spoken it aloud I knew that some details were best omitted.

It had been a catharsis to speak it all to someone though, an anonymous voice on the end of the line. But now here he was, in round spectacles and a pale grey suit. A young and eager journalist. A pivotal part of my still-solidifying plans.

"Do you believe me?" I ask, "About the ghosts?"

"I believe that you believe in them."

"An interesting response."

"Thank you. But you need evidence. You need more than suspicion, otherwise it'll just be another rumour story with nothing to back it up."

I smile then, as Irving draws himself handily into my plans, "Evidence." I say, "Or a confession?"

"From the horse's mouth, and nothing less. The De-Veire's are powerful, and no doubt would bring the full force of the law upon unfounded disparaging remarks against them."

"Then I will need your help."

Irving listens incredulously as I reveal my plan, and how he may fit into it. His bright eyes light up in excitement.

"Yes yes yes, absolutely." He agrees, giving me his full commitment.

"Thank you." I play with the lavender in my button-hole, "Thank you very much. Now, my errands."

He waves as I turn away from him, calling 'toodaloo'.

My arrival, next, at Nell's Place is fortuitous. As I walk up the narrow steps, who do I see at the top of the flight but the cowardly Doctor Mandelbaum. I hurry up behind him, and through into the back room, where Oddly is ensconced.

The little Doctor places his bag of medicines and syringes and other odd metal tools to one side, moving slowly over to the prone figure on the heaped mattresses and cushions. Oddly snores softly, and seems to be much restored. Mandelbaum's hands are shaking, and I watch quietly for a moment as he strokes the boy's face.

"How much will you charge for this unexpected house call?" I ask, making sure to keep emotion out of my voice. I must remain calm. I doubt the Doctor knew it was me that caused such a ruckus in the tunnel. It was too dark, and over too swiftly, for him to have had a clear look at me.

He jumps, squeaking slightly in alarm. Spinning around, he is tense and wild-eyed. I block his only means of escape, and I watch as he attempts to rally his wits.

"Just a courtesy, you understand." He says faintly, "I was in the area, and thought it best to call in and see how his recovery is progressing." His eyes linger on the floor. He doesn't like to look at me, "I have some new medicine..." Rushing to his bag, he fumbles it open, grabbing at a phial of clear liquid.

I move to his side, and he flinches at my proximity.

"May I see?"

Tentatively, slowly, uncertainly, he holds it out, but does not give it up. As I reach to take it he pulls away, toward Oddly.

"Leave it with me, Doctor." I say, putting some levity into my tone now. It isn't a command, not quite. He shoots me a viscous glare, and opens the phial.

"What's going on?" Lady Nell sweeps into her back room, distracting Mandelbaum enough for me to quickly step forward and snatch the phial.

"No! Please give it back." The small man is on the verge of tears, his face is pale and his lip quivers.

Nell stalks around the room, her eyes fixed upon Mandelbaum like those of a cat upon its prey.

"I hear tell that you've been a naughty boy." She wags a finger.

"Who told you that?" he asks.

Nell smiles in apology, "A Lady never tells."

"You appear to be in some distress, Doctor," I say, gesturing for him to sit, "I think I know someone who can help you."

He quakes, bereft, entirely unsure of himself, and with a great dread in his eyes. He fears Mr Nettle and Edward DeVeire enough to attempt murder, I remind myself, softening my tone, "All you have to do is talk to us."

"What do you know of my situation? Who do you know that could possibly help me?" He sits heavily, holding his face in pale, quivering hands.

"I know all about it. I was in the canal tunnel when you and Mr Nettle had your little chat."

Now his face snaps up to me, surprised and fearful.

"I didn't want to do it. Not any of it! They have been blackmailing me. Threatening me. I had to talk, or be killed too, or worse."

Selecting a china cup, Lady Nell scoops up a little of the gin from her bath tub and presses it into Mandelbaum's hands, "I think you need a drink."

She is right. He swallows the whole lot in two gulps, then gasps, and wipes the back of his sleeve across his mouth, "Thank you."

Slowly and clearly I explain to Nell and to Mandelbaum my plan. The Doctor is fretful, and refuses to take any part in it, whereas Nell claps her hands gleefully, giggling, excited! She sets about preparing at once, making notes and sending hastily scrawled letters to select individuals.

"What can I do to help?" Oddly sits up in Nell's bed,

he is awake, but slow and stiff.

I race over and hug him tightly, forcing him to wince. I forgot about his broken ribs, "Thank you." I say to him.

"For what?"

"For not dying. And for being there with Lawrie right at the end. So that he didn't die alone."

He doesn't ask me how I know, he simply acknowledges that I do. He holds my cheeks, staring into my eyes.

"Whatever stupid plan you have concocted, I want to play a part. I need to contribute."

He is still in a very poor state, and in no position to do much of anything aside from lay there and recover. But I yield, designating him the task of assisting Nell.

"I've always wanted a secretary." She smirks at the young prostitute, "Sure as eggs, we'll make a very efficient pair!"

Now Mandelbaum seems less wary, watching the three of us buoy one another with talk of success and the thought of less troublesome times ahead.

"You truly think I can be of assistance in your mad little scheme?" He ventures into a quiet moment.

I do, and tell him what he can do, if he feels up to it. He fidgets and plays his hands one over the other for several minutes, but finally he agrees.

"I must make amends." He says, "I must make amends."

I have one more person to visit this morning, and then everything will be prepared. *Mother Agapanthus' Gar-*

den Of Eden is a brothel I have been aware of for years, but never visited. It is one of the sort that charges extra for decorated rooms and clean bedding. It is also known for being an establishment where no appetite would be left wanting, so long as you paid the right price. From Lawrie's memories I knew that this is where he had worked to earn his money.

The door is innocuous enough, a simple dark wooden oblong set into a red brick facade. A small window is cut into the wall, the frosted glass hiding a red lantern, which illuminates during opening hours.

It is not lit now.

What might I find on the other side of this door? Beyond its simple rough surface lays a world Lawrie kept from me. A part of him that I did not know.

I knock on the door. I knock again and again, and loudly, until a very sleepy looking woman yanks open the door and screams 'what' in my face. She has the consistency of freshly kneaded dough, she smells of talc and other people's sweat.

"Mother Agapanthus?" I ask. But I know it is her. She is the angry woman from Lawrie's memory.

"If you're after a job you're out of luck." She says, looking me over with a lazy eye, "Plus, you're nothing special. Got four lads like you already. Unless you've got anything that'll set you apart? Contortionist? Twelve inch cock?"

"I'm not here for a job."

"Then what do you want, knocking me up so loud? You do know I work all night, don't you? I should be asleep right now, by rights. I *earn* my sleep!"

"I've come to ask you about Lawrence."

She tries to slam the door in my face, but I wedge my foot in so it cannot close. It is painful, and I will no doubt have a bruised little toe, but I need to speak to this woman.

"My name is Rowan, I want only to talk to you a while."

At the mention of my name she softens, squishy and plump, "Come in." She says, "Never thought I'd get to meet *you*."

I am taken into a small private sitting room where Mother Agapanthus brews up some very strong coffee. She pours herself a large cup and does not offer me any. I prefer tea anyway. Everything I have seen in this building so far is decorated in shades of red; the walls, the chairs, even the vases of fabric flowers are vivid shades of burgundy and scarlet.

The brothel madam pours herself into a deep armchair, looking for all the world like a dumpling in silk drawers, "So you are the famous Rowan." She shakes her head, "You've a lot to answer for."

"How so?"

Famous? I doubted that was the right word to use, and let the comment go unacknowledged.

"Lawrence worked for me for a few months before he met you. He was desperate when he turned up on my door. Destitute. He'd run away from home, of course you know all about that."

I confess that I have only recently learned a great many things about the Dear Departed. He kept a great deal to himself, or a secret from me at any rate, "He thought he was shielding me, protecting me."

Agapanthus sighs wistfully, "When he met you, at Nell's Place was it? Can't say as I've ever been. Not up all them steps, not with my knees. Well that was it. Smitten, he was. Love bug bit him good and hard."

The madam goes on in great deal for some time, revealing a part of Lawrie's life I have known nothing about.

He was resident at the brothel, kept a room where he lived and worked. He was a favourite with a lot of the punters.

"He was dashing and cocky and dynamite. We cater to all sorts here," She explains, "Got girls and boys and men and women and those of no fixed persuasion aboding under my roof. Only a handful stay for long. Passing through. Lawrence stayed longer than I expected, though."

Until one evening, that is, when someone called upon them for services of a most particular nature, and this person so scared Lawrence that he fled, and didn't return for two weeks. Agapanthus reveals that it was a visit from his brother. Edward had not called upon the house of sin because of Lawrence's presence, but to engage specific services.

"He wanted a boy, dressed as a girl, and wanted to be humiliated." The round woman speaks in a businesslike fashion. This is as common to her as jam and bread, but I can't deny I am taken aback. Surprised. Shocked, even.

"Edward is queer?"

"He used a false name, of course. And scurried out of here like a scalded cat once he finished."

"Quite a secret he's keeping there."

Could it be? That both DeVeire children turned out similarly anomalous in nature? I can only hypothesise, but where Lawrence had been at home with himself, Edward was not. His were feelings and passions alien to who he thought society instructed him to be. It made his killing of dear Lawrie all the sadder.

"He came back though," Agapanthus slurps at her coffee, "Lawrence did. Told us all about you. Wouldn't stop talking about you. He moved out of here to be with you. But then the letters started arriving."

"He told you about them?"

"Only mentioned them once. He'd had a few drinks. He was terrified of that brother of his. I got the impression he had been on the receiving end of a beating more than once." She shakes her head, "Poor lamb. And now he's six feet buried."

The door creaking open announces the arrival of several young men and women. The others who reside in the Garden of Eden. Their faces are pained, and determined. Can I fit these people and Mother Agapanthus into my plan?

Why yes, I do believe I can.

"I need your help."

The wheels are in motion and the cogs tick over on my scheme. We are going to put on a Ball! We have very little time, and so much to do, with so many of us having a part to play.

The thrill of it all keeps me sleepless for a week, until the predetermined date arrives. I prey to whichever deity may listen to the pleas of the queer, for us all to remain safe, and for us all to succeed in our private, vital missions.

Mandelbaum calls on me at home, nervous and sweating. He has disseminated the information I asked him to, and has had another, necessary run-in with the nefarious Mr Nettle.

He stands at the door to my room, reluctant to step inside, ringing his hands together, "Nettle is the one that savaged Oddly, and the crone. Tremblay went off back to France on very short notice, and so has been out of his reach. He now thinks that Oddly is dead, by my hand. I'm still beholden to him though, he knows too much about me."

"Don't worry." I say to him, smoothly, calming, "It all ends tonight."

"I hope so."

"He *does* know about the Ball?"

"Yes. I let slip about it, just as you instructed."

I thank the little Doctor, and he hurries away. My heart beats rapidly in my chest, nervous excitement rising in my stomach.

A waft of perfume rises up the stairwell and I am alerted to Tiffin's approach well before I see her.

"It was tricky. But It's done. You owe me."" She says,

a satisfied grin on her face.

"I don't doubt it."

I put on my best suit, the one made for me by Tremblay, dusting off the last of the soot stains that linger from the night of the DeVeire soiree.

The night is clear and a full moon hangs in the sky, a silver pendant upon a necklace of distant stars. Familiar streets take on a new and otherworldly sheen under Luna's gossamer touch, appearing frozen in time, one moment lingering on for longer than it ought, as I make my way on foot into Ancoates and the array of warehouses and mills within which we lay our trap.

My plan is a trap, a bringing together of everyone and everything involved in my life since dear Lawrie departed. Each of us a sharp tooth to close around Edward DeVeire and Mr Nettle as one great maw.

I watch as Taxicabs drop off attendees, others arrive on foot, and from within the old warehouse an up-tempo ragtime number can be heard.

I keep out of sight, and wonder where our victims might be. I doubt they are far, likely watching the same building as me, from some equally obtuse angle so as not to be seen.

Straightening up and adjusting my hair and jacket I make my way across the open road to the mill. I keep my eyes forward. I don't want to peer about for them. That would give the game away. My feet are inclined to go faster, they want to run into the building and my hands are eager to slam the door shut behind me. But I keep calm. I stride at a deliberately average speed, head held high, into the Mill.

I get a nod from Lady Nell. Everything is ready. There is a chair positioned in the centre of the large room, and I take up position in it, facing the doors.

Waiting.

Music plays loudly from a portable record player stashed at the rear of the room, and there are only a handful of candles lit about the vast space. They do a very poor job of illumination in this deep darkness. Aside from myself no one else can be seen. The attendees have been guided out of the rear of the venue and into another building two streets over for a real Ball.

I Wait. A sitting duck. Bait.

I keep my breathing low and steady, despite tension coiling up in me like a spring. I stare at the doors, willing them to open. The wait is excruciating. With every minute that passes, I fear our scheme has been discovered all the more. Perhaps Mandelbaum sold us out. Perhaps someone else gave something away. Maybe they aren't coming at all.

I drown out my doubts and worries with memories of Lawrence, and all that I have learned of him since he died. I feel his hand upon my shoulder now. Not physically, but in some other way. Some intangible ethereal way.

The doors crash open as Edward and Mr Nettle make their entrance. It is a brash and uncouth intrusion into the still of the Mill, and the emptiness that greets them brings them both up short. Their eyes dart about the darkness, wary, confused.

I knew they would not be able to resist. Mandelbaum had let slip just enough to entice them here, and more than enough to make them act foolishly together. Behind them the doors close and are locked. Edward fixes his animal stare on me, while Mr Nettle tries the door. It will not budge.

"What's the meaning of this?" Edward demands, shouting to be heard over the music.

The record finishes playing, and the hiss and crackle of the rotating disc fills the air. It is a soft, scratchy and discomforting sound.

Mr Nettle, now at his employers side, produces his knife, "Where are they?"

"Who?" I ask, remembering to keep my voice level.

"*Everyone*! We watched them come in here! Where have they gone?"

"Elsewhere. Having a lovely evening I hope."

Edward's expression is beginning to alter, his rage taking possession as I have seen before. I must play my hand carefully, "Why did you kill your brother?"

The hot-headed DeVeire pauses, his brows flicker in thought, "How do you know that?"

"You admit it was you?"

The knife glints in Mr Nettle's hand as he turns it slowly, rotating the blade, holding the point in my direction,

"Let's just do what we came here for. Off this runt, then it's done with."

I shake my head, "You killed your own brother because he was living a life you had forbidden yourself. You hated him, not because he was gay. But because *you* are, and are ashamed of it."

Edward's eyes widen, and his fists clench instinctively. His rage lingers, but now there is something else. He knows there is more to this encounter than meets the eye. He begins to stalk about, circling my chair. Mr Nettle remains in place. Damn. I can't keep them both in my line of sight simultaneously. I hope that Edward doesn't lose his cool before I have finished.

"What a lying little shit you are." Mr Nettle sneers at me, "A conniving, slimy little shit. The world is better off rid of your sort."

"And you," I turn my attention to the 'low sleuth' as Beloved Mother had called him, "Trying to tidy up after him. You were there when he killed Lawrie. Then you attempted to kill Oddly because he knew. Mandelbaum is a blabbermouth, isn't he? You followed the chain of Whisperers, trying to make sure that the truth wouldn't spread."

Shifty eyes dart left and right in Mr Nettle's wide head, scanning for an exit. For a way out.

"How do you know all this?" Edward booms, taking two heavy paces toward me. I flinch, but he comes no closer. Torn between beating me to a pulp, and getting information out of me, he is at an impasse. I can't tell him what he wants to know if I'm dead. I'm glad he realises this.

"A lady never tells." I jest, allowing some additional femininity into my tone and posture.

A mistake on my part, tipping him over the edge. He pelts forward, snarling and arms outstretched. A bear of a man, savage, primal, unleashed. The heat of his breath is upon my face, and the air moves as his bunched fists close in.

But the blows never land.

My eyes screwed shut, tight, I wait for the assault.

It never comes.

"What?..." Edward bellows and rages.

I open one eye, and peer up at him, his face flushed and red with blood and rage. He struggles to move, immobile, held by a hundred tiny hands.

The ghost children, emerging from the shadows at the last minute have restrained him. They put in very little effort, but across their vast number, their strength is impressive. They clutch at his clothes, and pinch his hair, and grab lumps of his skin.

Mr Nettle is struggling with the door, terrified.

"What unGodly thing is this!" He cries, looking over his shoulder at the snowball of children encasing Edward DeVeire, "Devils! Demons! Visions from Hell!"

I leave my chair and move to a safe distance from both men, "When the long dead ghosts of Manchester rise up against you, it's safe to say you've been a bad person. Admit what you have done. Say the words."

"How is this possible?" Edward rants and raves, pulling with one arm, then the other, struggling to break free of the spiritual embrace.

"Edward DeVeire, admit what you have done!" I

shout now, the chill thrill of retribution zipping up my spine.

"It's dirty! Disgusting! Unclean! He's better off dead. I did the world a favour!" Edward slavers, spitting his words, wild eyes hot as molten iron.

"Will that do as a confession?" I ask the darkness.

"That will do nicely." Replies Irving Periwinkle, emerging from the shadows. He makes notes in a little black book, recording the events of this evening and everything that is said.

"Who are you?" Mr Nettle rejoins the scene, finally giving up at the doors.

Irving smiles sweetly at the vicious man, "The name's Periwinkle. Journalist. This will make a sensational story for the morning edition, don't you think?"

"Only if you make it out of here alive." Mr Nettle darts forward, swift as a striking adder, but not so swift as Oddly Brown.

This is not part of the plan! Why is Oddly here?

"No!" I call out, fearful that my friend will not be up to a fight.

Even though he still suffers greatly, and his mobility is much diminished, he is quick as a flash and twice as nimble as Mr Nettle.

He wears beads and feathers in his hair, and carries a dagger to equal that of the low sleuth.

Taken by surprise, the would-be assassin has his knife knocked out of his grip, and stumbles. Oddly wastes no time, spinning on the spot, catching Mr Nettle between the ribs with his blade.

The vicious little man sags to the floor, wheezing as air escapes from his punctured lung. Oddly pulls free his knife, stained black with blood.

"That's not what we discussed!" I shout.

"I'm sorry. But he deserved it."

Mr Nettle is fast releasing a crimson tide across the floor.

"You'd best leave that part out." I say to Irving, who's face says he might not.

The record player is silenced, the hiss and crackle gone. The grunting and straining of Edward remains loud.

From the shadows Lady Nell and Saffron sweep across to the body of Mr Nettle, "We'll handle this." Nell says urgently, "We know the last rights he deserves." Between them they carry his body, dripping, away into the shadows.

Exhausting their powers of poltergeist, the children begin to fade. They fall away, piece by piece, into cobwebs and dust. Freed, Edward has had time to calm himself, and so stands glaring at me.

"What do you expect will happen now?" He asks, "I have friends at the Police, who will stand by my account of being ambushed by thieves in the night." He gestures around the room, knowing there are others lurking there, unseen, "I can have you disappear some other way. Though I will not find it as satisfying as the one I had envisioned for you." He cracks his knuckles.

Now it is the turn of Mother Agapanthus and a handful of her employees to step forward, "We know plenty about what satisfies you, my lad." She is dressed in ruffles and feathers, with a slit in her dress which reveals one pale, stockinged leg. She rests her weight on one foot, hand on hip.

"We have lots of wealthy clients. It'd be a bloody shame if we were to let slip what you like to get up to behind closed doors to all of them. All those *influential* men. Can't imagine they'd want much to do with you, what with your secrets all revealed, hmm?"

I see the beast return. Edward DeVeire can not hold his anger down for long, it seems. It bellows through him and as the focus of his ire, it is toward me that he advances. A demon raised from hell, he is thunder and billowing rage.

"Edward Kenneth DeVeire!" Beloved Mother's voice chimes like a rusty bell.

The large man freezes, stunned and suddenly scared. His face loses colour as blood drains from his cheeks.

"I have seen enough," She shuffles gently forward into the golden halo of one small candle, "As I think we *all* have."

The final person to move out of the darkness is the Desk Sergeant I have twice encountered at the Police Station. Edgar's contact there, and as I learned from Saffron only a few days ago, is a distant cousin of his.

"You're nicked." He says, matter of fact.

Held immobile and diminished under Beloved Mother's gorgon stare, Edward can do nothing but mutter whimpering platitudes.

The Sergeant slaps cuffs onto his wrists, and using his baton as encouragement, leads the larger man out of the Mill and into a waiting carriage.

CHAPTER TWELVE

A NEW ROOM MATE

"Like glittering lights on the surface of pond scum, you lot. You make the grime worth bearing." Edgar pulls on his jacket.

The Constables around us watch uneasily as he dons male regalia. He laughs again in disbelief, shaking his head. Nell, Saffron and myself brought him a copy of the morning edition, the front page of which is covered by Irving's article. He has thankfully stuck to the main meat of the story, leaving the peculiar trimmings unmentioned.

The Desk Sergeant pats Edgar on the back as he passes, and Edgar nods politely. He is being released. Strings have been pulled and someone very high up has been paid off. It is not an ideal situation Edgar is released into, but better than it could have been.

"Luckily I still own some family property I can sell." He says, "Now that business may not be what it was." He takes Saffron's hand and they walk proudly out of the Station.

Nell links her arm into mine, watching them go.

"Epitome of class, those two." She remarks, "Cream of the crop."

I agree.

"Has your lover boy shown his face since last night?"

"No. I thought he might have done. I hoped he would. But no."

"Perhaps his unfinished business is finished now?"

"Yes, perhaps."

I can hear Edward DeVeire making loud threats and thumping about in a cell somewhere close by, and excuse myself to pay him a visit.

I need to make sure. I need to see him locked up.

I need to know we're safe.

He tosses himself about like a great ape, banging his fists upon the walls. I think that he is a sorry sight. He has lost all semblance of his Gentlemanly persona, stripped back, layers of carefully manicured veneer peeled away to reveal the terrified and bitter creature within.

Upon seeing me, he pushes himself at the bars, reaching through, pointing a finger in my direction, "You will be sorry you made an enemy of a DeVeire, *faggot*!"

Beloved Mother appears at my shoulder, and Edward stiffens, "I thought you were raised better than this." She displays great disappointment, her small dark eyes are wet and sad, "I hope you are ashamed of what you have done."

Miraculously Edward finds his voice, the barrier of bars somehow deflecting away a portion of Narcissus DeVeire's power over her son, "I am ashamed only that I could not finish what I started."

This retaliation cuts his Mother to the quick. She raises her head, sucking back her emotions and becoming distant. She gazes at her son for a long time, silent, her expression withering, blank and cold.

"There was a time when I had two sons. It seems to me they both died on the night of that terrible murder. I do not know who or what you are." She reaches out to me, "My family lays in ruins, thanks to you." Her words are harsh and unexpected, "I shall be leaving Manchester for good, retiring to my family estate in north Wales."

She turns to go, looking at me strangely over her shoulder, "Perhaps you would like to visit me now and again? I think I might like the company."

But she isn't looking at me.

She is looking at the Dear Departed. Standing at my side, he pushes his hand into mine, holding it tightly. His mother's eyes dart to our clasped hands for a moment, and she almost smiles. She leaves then, shuffling on ancient feet out of my life.

"Lawrence?" Edward slurs, disbelieving.

The Dear Departed releases my hand and takes a step toward his brother, "I forgive you." He says, then vanishes.

As I leave, Edward cries out, but now his utterances shift from a song of rage, to sorrow and mourning. He thrashes about like a caged animal, wailing, gibbering, and howling.

"I've heard whispers that the poor DeVeire fellow is being packed off to a Sanitarium. Seems he's been raving about ghosts and all manner of strange things." Nell says to me as we sit at her bar.

"And who did you hear that from?" I ask.

She taps her nose with an elegant finger, keeping schtum.

"One thing I meant to ask before. What did you and Saffron do with Mr Nettle?"

Once more she taps her nose, keeping her secrets locked away, "Best not to ask. Quite unceremonious."

"He's gone now, I think." I say after a while, "It's been a month and Lawrie hasn't been back."

I had of course told her about his final words to Edward at the Police Station, and she nods sagely, "I wonder what the gin's like in heaven."

I laugh at her, and the evening progresses jovially, as an evening ought to at Nell's Place. Conversation turns around on itself, pivoting across all manner of disjointed topics, until the subject of my accommodation comes up yet again.

"Don't worry about me," I say, "I've had my locks changed and found a new lodger to share my room and my bills."

Nell is taken aback, "Oh yes indeed? Who?"

"Oddly."

She nods, an agreeable smile on her bright lips.

"Though his real name is Inteus, did you know that?"

"I did not!" Lady Nell is loath to admit.

"It means 'someone who has no shame', or some similar thing, apparently."

"Sure as eggs, that's Oddly!"

I lied to her. I have a secret to keep. The Dear Departed has not departed. In fact he has been making more appearances of late, now that whatever ethereal obstruction lay before him has been lifted. He can't tell me much about what lays beyond life, he doesn't remember clearly anything of when he isn't haunting me. His visitations are... exciting.

And it seems my days as a fae Holmes are not done with. I have been approached by a young woman, a fragile little person, pale as milk and wavering like a leaf caught in a gale; seeking help.

News of me and my spectral assistants bringing down the ferocious Edward DeVeire seems to have spread wide amongst the queer demimonde, and now I have been sought out.

Perhaps there's money to be made as an independent investigator with a ghost for a partner? And perhaps there's some adventures to be had by a lavenderist like me, with a ghost for a lover.

ALSO AVAILABLE FROM
RYLAN JOHN CAVELL

The Department Of Lost Things

Utterly Bewildered

The Blood Moon

Tattoos By Rylan *(a colouring book)*

The Strange Adventures Of Professor Calamity

Printed in Poland
by Amazon Fulfillment
Poland Sp. z o.o., Wrocław